a greater goode

a greater goode

a novel by
amy schor ferris

Houghton Mifflin Company
Boston 2002

www.houghtonmifflinbooks.com

The text of this book is set in 12.5-point Adobe Garamond.

Library of Congress Cataloging-in-Publication Data
Ferris, Amy Schor
A greater Goode / by Amy Schor Ferris.
p. cm.
Summary: Twelve-year-old Addie worries about spending a summer without her best friend Luke and about the fate of an unwed pregnant woman who does not seem to have anywhere to go.
ISBN 0-618-13154-X
[1. Best friends—Fiction. 2. Friendship—Fiction. 3. Mother and child—Fiction. 4. Unmarried mothers—Fiction. 5. Pregnancy—Fiction. 6. Pennsylvania—Fiction.]
PZ7.F374 Gr 2002   [Fic]—dc21   2001039234

Manufactured in the United States of America

QUM 10 9 8 7 6 5 4 3 2 1

This book is lovingly dedicated to

Marianne Moloney, Daisaku Ikeda, Margaret Raymo,
Linda Johnson, Paula Miksic, Sonda Miller,
Kristi Zea, Sheri Myers, Steven Sater, James Lecesne,
Randy Levinson, Sjoerd DeJong, Bob Topol,
Tony Trotta, Kevin Haddad, Melinda Rosenthal,
Patricia Elam, Kathy Aiken, Terri, Helen, Sara, Kiersten,
Dorothy, Obelah, B.J., Ruth, and all the Divas.
Juli, Allison, Deb, Monica, Sean Cooley, Peter Werner,
Robert Forte, Ted Fujioka, Richard Sonoda, Eric Hauber,
Bruce, Grayce, Aaron, and Erica.

Willow Lindley, who was the inspiration for Addie.

Ken Ferris, who is simply my inspiration.

My mom and Sam Schor. I miss you, Daddy.

prologue

My best friend, Luke, he told me to write this story. Luke's like a genius, you know, like that guy Stephen . . . what's his name? You know, the guy that's in the wheelchair, and he talks through a tube or somethin'. You know who I'm talkin' about? It'll come to me—stuff like that always does. I just gotta go through the alphabet . . . that's what I do when I can't remember someone's name . . . I go through the alphabet. My grandma, she taught me that. Anyway, Luke's like that guy, except he's not in a wheelchair. He's just real smart. He's sorta quiet, except when he's talkin' about the universe and all sorts of stuff that I hardly understand, but he's my best friend in the whole world, and he told me that I should sit down and tell you my story.

My name's Addie Goode. I'm twelve years old, and I live in Lumberland, Pennsylvania, with my dad. His name's Myles, and he's the best dad anyone could ever have. Honest. When I was three years old, my mother, she just up and left us. Like that. She wrote my dad a letter. All it said was "Dear Myles, I can't take it anymore, not you, not the kid, nothing. I just can't take it anymore. Sarah." When I was old enough to read, I found the letter stuffed in the bottom of his drawer. It was all wrinkled, like he had crumpled it up and was gonna throw it out but had second thoughts. I found it and I read it and I hated my mother from that day on. I just hated her. My dad and me, we lived in Fayetteville, Georgia, back then. We had this condo on the lake. It had two bedrooms, and I could see the water from my room. After a few years, my dad decided that we oughta move. I think he kept waitin' for her to come back to be with us, but she never did. She never called or wrote or anything. He said it got to be real hard breathin' in that apartment. For a while I thought maybe he had some lung problem, like asthma, but I think it was that he just couldn't stand bein' reminded of her. We moved to Lumberland. We have a real nice house with a barn in the back. We live right by the Delaware River. In the summer, me and Luke, we go to the river and walk on the stones, and sometimes when it's real hot, we take a blow-up raft and just float. He talks about the universe and the stars and stuff like that. I just daydream, and when Luke's all finished talkin', I just look at him and say, "Wow, that's cool."

A, B, C, D, E, F, G, H—Hawkings, that's his name, Stephen Hawkings. See that, it works all the time. Maybe it's Hawkins, I don't really know for sure. I just know he's one of those geniuses. Like Einstein.

Anyway, this is my story. It all happened a coupla months ago, right after Halloween.

chapter one

I had the worst stomachache. Me and Luke, we ate almost all the candy we got trick-or-treatin'. It was sorta like a contest. We went up to my barn and scattered all the candy on the floor. I musta ate twenty-five Reese's peanut butter cups. I don't think I'm ever gonna eat peanut butter again. Ever. Luke got so sick, he threw up—stuck his head out the barn window and just threw up. I hadda walk him home, 'cause he was so sick and his mother, Joyce—she's the bartender at Pete's Bar—had made Luke promise he wouldn't eat any candy until after his dentist's appointment. Luke's dad, Charlie, he teaches at the high school. He and Joyce are separated, except they spend every Saturday night together. Luke says they're tryin' to work things out, which I think is a good thing, since I like them both. Anyway, Luke made this promise and didn't keep it, and Joyce was gonna throw a fit.

"You gotta walk me home, Addie. My mom's gonna take one whiff of me, and she's gonna know I got sick 'cause I ate so much candy."

"You want me to lie for you, Luke?"

"Uh-uh, just walk me home."

When we got to Luke's house, all the lights were out, except for the porch light, which meant that Joyce wasn't home yet. It's those kinda miracles in life make you believe. I don't believe much in God, but when stuff like that happens, it makes you wonder.

Minute I got home, I put on my pajamas, brushed my teeth, and got right into bed. All night long, my stomach was hurtin' and achin', and I tossed and turned. I didn't get hardly any sleep. I keep a light on at night, right by my bed, 'cause bein' in the dark scares me. Always has. When I got up in the mornin' to go to school, I musta been white as a ghost, 'cause Jessie—she takes care of me and my dad, cooks the meals, cleans the house, keeps everything smellin' fresh—she told me I should stay home from school.

"You look like Casper, child, just pitiful."

Jessie's my second-best friend in the whole world. She's got the prettiest color skin—it looks like cocoa with some milk in it—and she wears her hair all up in a knot on top of her head. And every single mornin', no matter what time she shows up, she's wearin' a face full of makeup. "Never leave home without a pair of pretty panties on and lips full of red." That's what she says. And she wears the coolest clothes—makes them herself. She goes to the fabric store, and whatever fabric's on sale, she buys it. Then she sews up a storm. She got my dad to buy her a used sewin' machine. When she first came to our house, sorta like an interview, she just walked around noddin', her hands on her hips, noddin' noddin' noddin'. You woulda thought *she* was interviewin' *us*. "You want me takin' care of your child, and your meals, and keepin' your house tidy, I want two hundred a week cash and a sewin' machine." Sometimes she makes me a skirt or blouse when she has leftovers.

"I bet you ate up all those goodies, bet you stuffed 'em in your mouth, like you were on fire or somethin'."

"Me and Luke, we coulda opened a candy store."

"Instead, you ate all the merchandise. I'm gonna make you some oatmeal, bind your stomach, then I want you goin' up to your room and stayin' in bed."

"I'm not that sick."

Jessie poured some Quaker Oats into a saucepan and stood over the stove.

"Dad leave already?"

"Uh-huh. He hadda be at court real early this mornin'. Wants to see if Judge Thompson'll suspend Toby Rogers's sentencing. That fool shoulda kept his hands in his pockets. He just likes swingin' at everybody, don't he?"

She placed the oatmeal down on the table, right in front of me. I hate oatmeal. I hate the way it looks. I hate the way it smells. I most especially hate the way it tastes.

"Can I have some honey?"

Jessie just stood lookin' at me.

3

"Please."

Jessie always says if you don't say please or thank you, it shows a lack of graciousness. "Polite breeds polite"—that's what she always says.

"Who did Toby hit?"

"He got into a disagreement with that fella works at the Texaco station, I forget his name. You know who I'm talkin' about?"

"Why don't you go through the alphabet? Works for me."

"You and the alphabet—it ain't gonna get you in college."

"What makes you think I wanna go to college? Maybe I wanna travel the world. That sounds like more fun."

"Fun don't make money. Fun's what you do when you have money, and you gotta go to school to become somethin' so that you can earn a good livin' and then spend it on whatever you want."

"You go to college, Jessie?"

"See that, I'm a prime example. No, I did not go to college. You think if I went to college, I'd be cleanin' houses, watchin' after you? Luther, that's the guy's name. Luther—and I didn't use the alphabet, missy. Anyway, Toby was gettin' irritated that Luther was takin' so long to get to his tank. Seems Luther was chattin' it up with some other fella when Toby pulled in and paid no attention to Toby, and that just sorta did it for him. Toby got outta his car and told Luther he wanted a fill-up. When Luther continued to pay no attention, Toby punched him in the face, and there was blood drippin' all down his Texaco shirt.

"So Judge Thompson, he gave Toby thirty days in county jail. I think your daddy's pissin' in the wind on this one. Ain't no way Judge Thompson is gonna suspend nothin'. I told your daddy this mornin', 'You are pissin' in the wind.'"

"What'd he say to that?"

"He said, 'Someone's gotta piss in the wind, Jessie.'" She sat down at the table, pushed the oatmeal closer to me. "It's gettin' cold, Addie."

"I don't wanna eat this. You eat it." I pushed it across the table, right in front of her. "I'm gonna make myself some eggs."

"Eggs ain't gonna do it, oatmeal, oatmeal's what binds your stomach, but don't listen to me, Addie."

"I listen to you all the time, Jessie."

"Uh-huh. You listen, child, but you don't hear. Hearin's what's important. Fine by me—you go make yourself some eggs." She stood up. Jessie's the type, when you don't agree with her, she gets all pissy. "I got laundry to do, and then I'm gonna sew myself a pretty party dress."

"What happens when you piss in the wind, Jessie?"

She turned to me. "It comes right back and smacks you in the face." Then she looked down at herself. "I think a nice hot-pink party dress will do the trick for my date Saturday. Fine fella, real fine fella."

Jessie loves men. Says they're the flowers on the surface of the earth. She's always got a new man in her life. Now Lumberland is pretty small, everyone knows everyone, and most people have lived here most of their lives. She's gone through pretty much all the available men in this town. She's even gone through a few of the husbands, and the reason I know this is 'cause Charlie, Luke's daddy, was one of 'em. Me and Luke, we cut outta school one day. There was this fair comin' to the next town, and we wanted to see the animals they were bringin' in, so we cut school and went over to Luke's house to pick up some money to take the bus. And there in the living room, wrapped like two pieces of cord, were Charlie and Jessie. Me and Luke, we just stood there, holdin' our breath. I thought Luke's eyes were gonna pop right out of the socket.

"You okay, Luke?" I asked in a whisper.

He turned to me and covered his mouth with his hand. I could tell he was gigglin'. Now why he thought that was funny, I don't really have a clue, 'cause if Charlie were my dad, I wouldn't be laughin'. We musta been standin' there an awfully long time, 'cause Jessie turned from the couch and caught us with her eyes. That's when Luke and me, we ran outta the house. Jessie never said a word to me, and I never said a word to her. But someone musta said a word or two to Joyce. Two days later, she threw Charlie outta the house. Luke told me that she put all Charlie's clothes in Hefty bags and placed 'em in the front yard with a note pinned to 'em: GO TO HELL CHARLIE AND TAKE YOUR CLOTHES WITH YOU.

I don't know who Jessie has a date with on Saturday night, but I know for sure it can't be Charlie, 'cause he and Joyce are tryin' to mend their marriage.

chapter two

Me and Luke, we both stayed home from school. He was throwin' up all night. When Luke misses school, it don't mean much. When I miss school, it's sorta like I fall behind six months. Everything I learn the day before goes right through me. My dad says when it comes to school, some people are like sponges and others are like toilet bowls. I'm the toilet bowl type. I just get bored, that's all. I mean really, honestly, what am I gonna be usin' arithmetic for? I look at it this way: When I get old enough and have my own checkin' account, I'm either gonna be in a plus or a minus. And now that they have all sorts of stuff, like . . . What's it called? I know Jessie has it, 'cause she's always callin' the bank and yellin' at 'em. A, B, C, D, E, F, G, H, I, J, K, L, M, N, O—got it. Overdraft. Works every time. With stuff like that, who really needs arithmetic? Anyway, bein' that

Luke stayed home and I stayed home, he came over, and we watched TV and played cards. And bein' that it was Friday, it was sorta like havin' a three-day weekend, like Memorial Day or somethin'.

We were watchin' some TV show, like a talk show, and it was all about marriage. It was kinda weird. The TV host was sayin' that if women don't get married by the time they're thirty-five years old, chances are real slim they're ever gonna. Now personally, I'm not plannin' to get married for a real long time. I figure by the time I'm forty, I'll be ready.

"You ever think about gettin' married, Luke?"

"Uh-uh, not lately."

"I don't mean now, Luke. I mean, what age you wanna be when you get married?"

Luke and me, we never ever talk about stuff like this, 'cause we're just kids, but when you're watchin' a TV show like that, it crosses your mind, I guess.

"Luke, you wanna have kids when you get married?"

"I don't know, maybe."

"Well, I'm gonna have five or six, I'm gonna have a lot of babies, but I'm definitely not gonna breast-feed 'em. Wanna know why?" Luke sorta nodded. I could tell this was of no interest to him. "Jessie told me her sister, her younger sister, she had two babies, and her breasts, they almost hung to her knees. She said her breasts hung so low that she couldn't even walk straight. I can't even imagine what that musta looked like."

"*National Geographic* always has pictures of tribal women. They have breasts like that. They look like long sacks."

I can always count on Luke to gimme an answer like that. "Well, I'm just gonna feed 'em with a bottle and not worry about any physical harm done to me. I'm hungry. You hungry?"

Luke and me, we took the river road to town. All the trees were gray and bare. You could tell by lookin' at the sky that pretty soon winter would be comin'. When it snows here, everything is covered like a blanket of white. Sometimes we get fifteen inches of snow in one fall. Everything freezes, the trees all sparkle with icicles, and at night, when the moon is full or almost, everything looks like glass. But now it's just dreary and gray. Can't say it's pretty, just sorta bland. Luke was quiet on our walk.

"Whatcha thinkin' about, Luke?"

"The afterlife."

See, this is what I mean. Most boys his age think about sports or girls or music. Not Luke. He's in his own world. Lukeland, that's what I call it, Lukeland.

"You wanna talk about it, Luke? Cause I don't really wanna talk about it, but if you wanna talk about it, I'll listen. I just won't contribute."

"You ever wonder where people go after they die, Addie?"

Now I wasn't gonna contribute, but that seemed like an easy one. "I guess heaven or hell. That's my guess."

9

"I don't think so. I don't think that's where people go. I think heaven or hell is inside of people."

I gotta say, havin' given it some thought, Luke could be right. But whaddya do with information like that?

Luke and me, we went to the luncheonette in town. Dottie and Sy's Luncheonette, that's what it's called. I had a grilled cheese sandwich, and Luke had a tuna melt. Dottie and Sy, they gotta be in their seventies. She moves so slow, you gotta order your food the minute you walk in the door. And Sy, he's hard of hearin'. Unless you scream, he can barely hear you. He's always sayin', "What?" or "What's that you say?" They've been married forever, and they still like each other. He'll come up to her when she's by the grill and pinch her butt. They have magazines and candy and let you read the magazines without buyin' 'em. Except, of course, if you're a stranger and then they make you buy what you're readin'. So Luke and me, we took some magazines off the rack and sat at the counter, eatin' and readin'. I wasn't really readin'. I was lookin' at the pictures. *Glamour* magazine. Sometimes I wish I was as pretty as a model, all slinky and posin'.

After we ate and looked through all the magazines we wanted, we headed up Broad Street. Broad Street is like Main Street in other towns, everything on one street and that is pretty much the entire town of Lumberland. You got the barbershop, which is run by Paul Farley. He's probably in his forties. His daddy owned the barbershop, but he died and Paul took over. Paul is big and fat; his thighs rub to-gether when he walks. And he sprays himself all over with cologne, whoa . . . I'm tellin' you, you get real close, and you wanna hold your nose. But I really like him. He talks and talks and talks—Mr. Chatty Cathy—and except for his smell, I think he's awfully nice.

"Well, hello, Addie Goode." Paul always comes outta the shop if no one's there or he's not busy.

"Hey, Paul." I can't say much more than that, 'cause I try and hold my breath.

"I started goin' to the gym, you know, the one down in Hawley . . . hey, Luke." Luke held his breath, too, and nodded hello. Paul kept on goin'. "My doctor says I gotta lose at least fifty pounds. So I go to the gym, right? And it's got all the newest equipment, so I get on this Nautilus ma-chine without checkin' anything out, and I'm on the ma-chine no more than ten minutes—ten minutes tops—and the whole thing collapses right from under me. The whole thing just crashed. There was this sign I neglected to read, right above the machine. It said no one over 250 should use it. I'm weighin' in now at 287. The whole machine, like it crumpled right under me. The gym, they're makin' me pay for it. Eight hundred dollars! Every single week, a hundred outta my check."

See what I mean? Mr. Chatty Cathy. His string gets stuck.

"Whaddya gonna do now?"

"I guess I'll do pushups in the privacy of my home."

"Maybe you oughta try push-aways."

"Never heard of that, push-aways."

"Push away the plate in front of you! That's my dad's form of exercise. Push-aways."

Paul patted me on the head. First it was sorta gentle, then it got a little harder, like the way he was laughin'.

"Push-aways. I like that; that's funny. I'm gonna try that. That's a good one . . . That's a good one."

A coupla doors down from Paul, you have a few antique stores. I never go in 'em. Luke sometimes does. He likes things that are old and were owned by other people. He says they got history. But I don't like history much. It's another subject I don't do well in.

Then you have this pretty flower shop. It's called Floral Design. The windows are always full of fresh flowers: roses, tulips, lilacs. And the woman who owns that store, her name is Grayce. And she and my dad, they're sorta in like. My dad says she's a breath of fresh air. Grayce is real pretty. She's got long, dark hair; she wears it up when she's workin' and wears it down when she's with my dad. She moved to Lumberland three years ago. She was married, and her husband died. I think it was a freak accident. That's what I overheard her sayin' one day. He was thirty-eight years old, and now I'm tryin' to remember exactly what she said when I overheard her. I think she said he was drivin' home, and the weather was real bad—it was stormin' and rainin' and the wipers on his car weren't workin' all that well—and he drove right into a stone wall. Smashed the car and himself to bits. Anyway, she moved here from Boston and opened her shop. My dad went in one day to buy his secretary flowers for her birthday, and I guess he and Grayce really liked each other. But my dad, he's sorta . . . What's that word I'm lookin' for? It starts with the letter G, I think. A, B, C, D, E, F, G . . . Huh, this one's a hard one. It'll come to me; it always does. One day, me and Jessie we were talkin'—we had just left the flower shop—and we were talkin' about Grayce and my dad.

"Your dad's been burned real bad once, and you know, once you rub your hand up against a hot stove, you keep a fair distance from that appliance, no matter how shiny and nice it looks."

"You like her, Jessie?"

"I like her plenty. She makes your daddy happy, and when Myles is happy, I'm happy."

"I guess I like her, too."

For a long time, my dad, he wasn't very happy. He would sit around, wearin' misery like Paul wears cologne. But since he's known Grayce, you could just tell he's feelin' different about things. When Grayce's got someone in the store, I just wave. But when she's alone, I go in and say hi.

Then there's the dentist's office. I've only been in there a coupla times, for cavities, but I don't like the dentist or his office, so I don't wanna talk about that. Then you got the Texaco station, with Luther, who's wearin' a bandage on his nose. Then you got the drugstore, the bank, and the new church that sits on the corner of Broad and Mill. It's caused a lot of trouble, and I don't wanna talk about that right now either. Then you got Pete's Bar, but there isn't anyone named Pete, so I don't know where the name came from.

And then down the street, there's my dad's office. A sign hangs out front. It says, MYLES GOODE, ATORNEY AT LAW. Now I know what you're thinkin'. There are two *t*s in attorney. But I made that sign in camp a coupla years ago, when I was nine, and I misspelled the word. But he liked it so much, he hung it outside. I think that tells you a whole lot about my dad.

Luke and me, we went to visit him. Cheryl, his secretary, she's sorta strange. She's in her twenties, and she wears her hair all short and spiky, and every coupla weeks, it's a different color. This week it's purple. She wears a nose ring and has three tattoos, two on her arm and one on her ankle. You can't see the tattoos, except in the summer when she's sleeveless and wearin' sandals. She told me once if I ever wanted a tattoo, she'd take me to the place where she got 'em. Bein' that I hate needles, chances are pretty slim I'd ever get a tattoo. But if I ever did, I'd get a little, tiny rose right on my shoulder.

"Hey, Addie. Hey, Luke."

"Hey, Cheryl."

"You here to see Myles?"

"Uh-huh."

14

"He's on the phone. Be a few minutes. Why don't you just sit down, make yourselves at home." She was readin' a magazine, some motorcycle magazine. I looked over her shoulder. "You ever been on a motorcycle, Addie?"

"Nope. Just a convertible."

"I'm gonna buy a motorcycle. I'm savin' up, and when I get it, you and me, we're gonna go for a ride."

"How much they cost?"

"A lot of money. But I'm figurin' if I can't save up enough, maybe I can get a loan. Your dad's off the phone. Why don't you just go in." When Luke walked by her she said, "You're quiet, aren't you?" He nodded.

Now I know this is gonna sound prejudiced, but my dad is the best-lookin' guy in the whole world. He's tall, and when he smiles, he makes you feel like you swallowed the sun. And he's got the bluest bluest eyes, like the sky when it's clear.

"Jessie tells me you stayed home from school, says you were sick."

"I was, but I'm better now."

"I can see. You, too, Luke, you stayed home?"

"I was throwin' up all night, Mr. Goode."

"How many times I have to tell you, you can call me Myles? What kinda trouble you two gettin' into today, other than not goin' to school?"

"Did the judge throw out Toby's sentence?"

"Nope. Toby's gonna be stayin' in the county jail for

thirty days. He'll probably get himself in trouble in there, too. You just gotta look at him cross-eyed, and that'll do it. He's got a real mean streak."

"Me and Luke, we were talkin' earlier, and I wanna ask you somethin'. You believe in the afterlife, Dad?"

Luke got all red from blushin'. My dad thought about this for a minute. I can always tell when my dad's thinkin', 'cause he rubs his chin.

"That's a pretty serious subject, Luke."

"Uh-huh." That's all Luke said.

"Luke says he don't believe people go to heaven or hell when they die, says he thinks that's inside of people, like their feelin's. You think that's true?"

My dad looked straight at Luke. "I think that's true. What do I always tell you, Addie? I always say you can look in someone's eyes and see their life. When I look in Toby's eyes, I see a man full of hate. When I look in your eyes, I see sweetness. So I guess if you can see someone's life in their eyes, you can tell the condition of their soul. Some people live in hell, and some live in heaven."

Luke was feelin' better, not so embarrassed anymore. My dad has a way of makin' people feel good about themselves.

"So do you believe in the afterlife then, Dad?"

"I'll tell you what. I'll tell you what I know. It certainly isn't somethin' I think about much. All I worry about is right now."

The phone rang. It musta rang five times before Cheryl

16

picked it up. She stuck her head in my dad's office. "Judge Thompson's on the phone. Says there's a crisis."

"Always a crisis with Judge Thompson. That's how he gets me to answer the phone." My dad gave me a kiss and a hug goodbye. Then he shook Luke's hand. "I gotta get back to work, Addie. I'll see you later."

"You havin' supper with Grayce tonight?"

"I'm takin' her out to dinner."

"Then I'm gonna have supper at Luke's." I turned to Luke. "Can I have supper with you tonight?"

"I guess."

When we walked out of my dad's office, Cheryl was polishin' her nails. I leaned over the desk. She was makin' a mess of it. The polish was mostly gettin' on her skin. A lime green color with sparkles. Hideous.

"Halloween's over, Cheryl."

"You just don't have any fashion sense, Addie." She held up her hand and waved it at me. "This is the newest color." Then the phone rang, and she sorta ignored it, until my dad yelled from his office, "Could you answer the phone, Cheryl? Please?"

She blew on her nails and picked up the phone. "Myles Goode, Attorney at Law. How can I help you?"

Gun-shy. That's the word. My dad's gun-shy. That's what Jessie says he is.

chapter three

Luke and me, we kept walkin'. Musta walked two miles outta town. We went to the Kmart in the strip mall. Talk about an ugly piece of real estate. It's flat, and all the stores in the strip mall, they're painted a dirty white color. Anyway, the Kmart has video games. So we pooled our change and played for a few hours.

Now right next to the video games is a Domino's Pizza, sorta connected to the Kmart inside. I couldn't help but notice this couple sittin' there, it seems like they were in the middle of a fight. You know, the type when two people aren't talkin' to each other, but there's real anger between 'em. She looked like maybe nineteen, twenty, and she had a belly full of baby. Looked like she was ready to pop any minute. Her hair was long and stringy, and her mascara was all smudged under her eyes, like a raccoon. He was probably a little older than her, and he was all skinny and jittery and kept gettin' up and down from his chair. Up and down, up and down—made you dizzy just watchin'. He had the meanest face. Sometimes you pick up things about people for no reason really except you notice 'em. Thing I noticed about him, his nails, his fingernails were all bit down, like he chewed on 'em. Anyway, I kept lookin' at 'em out of the corner of my eye. Somethin' musta happened—she musta gotten him real mad—'cause he threw a slice of pizza right at her, hit her in the face.

"You lousy nothin'." He was cursin' and screamin' so loud everyone, includin' Luke, just stared at him. When he walked out of Domino's, he just stopped and stared right at me. Long and hard, like his eyes were goin' through my body. I got the chills; my arms were all full of goose bumps. And then he stormed outta there.

I turned to Luke and said, "Was that the creepiest guy ever?"

The girl, she just sat there, shakin' her head; her eyes started to fill. I guess she was embarrassed, everyone lookin' at her. I felt real sorry for her—bein' pregnant and all, havin' him cursin' loud—but I decided to mind my own business, even though somethin' was tellin' me she could use a friend.

"Not everyone needs a friend, Addie. Sometimes people just wanna be left alone. You're just gonna have to start mindin' your own business and let people be." My dad always says that to me, and let me tell you why. Coupla years ago, I started bringin' home stray dogs and cats. I would hide 'em in the barn, so my dad and Jessie wouldn't know, and I would bring table scraps to feed 'em. Well, one night the doorbell rang, and it was Pauline Trumbull. She lives across the river, she reminds me of the Wicked Witch. One of those women who never got married and fills her house with cats and dogs, that type. Anyway, make a long story short, she stood on our front porch, and she demanded to know where her pets were.

"What are you talkin' about, Pauline?"

"My pets, Myles. I let 'em out in my yard, and now they're missin'. You seen 'em?"

My dad was in a foul mood that evening. I had just gotten my report card, and three out of five teachers wrote, "Losing interest and performing poorly." I had tried to get the report card out of the mailbox before my dad, thinkin' I could hide it from him, but he caught the mailman before I did. I was up in my room, bein' punished, when I heard Miss Trumbull's voice boomin' from the porch.

"You sure you didn't see my pets?"

I came out of my bedroom and stood at the top of the stairs. "They're in the barn, Miss Trumbull."

Both my dad and Miss Trumbull turned to look at me. My dad had one of those looks on his face that said, *You're in deep, deep trouble, Addie.*

I went out to the barn with my dad and Miss Trumbull. Her pets were asleep, all curled up with each other on this blanket I had put out for them. A Tupperware bowl was filled with water.

Miss Trumbull gathered her pets and didn't say a word to either my dad or me. A thank you woulda been nice for takin' such good care of 'em, but Miss Trumbull doesn't have very much graciousness to her.

When we got back in the house, that's when my dad told me about mindin' my own business.

The girl just sat there. I figured she was waitin' for that creep to come back. And he did. I just hadda feelin' he would. He didn't say anything to her, and she didn't say anything to him. He pulled her up real hard from the chair, and it looked like he was draggin' her out. I made it a point to look at her. I offered her a kind smile. I know she saw me, 'cause she nodded at me. A smile wasn't gonna be easy for her, which was okay. Sometimes givin' a smile is a whole lot better than gettin' one.

Me and Luke, we took the long way home. It was startin' to get dark. Not pitch-dark, but the kinda sky where the blue and the gray blend together. A little more than day, and a little less than night. We took the back road, which sorta leads you into the woods. There's this path goes from the woods to the river, and then you walk over a little, tiny wooden bridge. Anyway, that's the road we took.

"You think I'm ever gonna do better than Cs and C minuses in school?"

"I think you gotta open a book, Addie, and then you gotta read it."

"I don't see you openin' many books, Luke. Why's that?"

"I have a photographic memory. I can look at somethin' once and remember it forever."

"What kinda brain is that?"

"I just retain things."

"Like a sponge. What kinda brain you think I got? What kinda memory?"

"Short-term."

Now there's this church that's all closed down in the woods. Remember I told you about that church in town, the new one? Well, this church needed fixin' up, 'cause it was all old and fallin' apart, and some people in town wanted to fix it, make it all nice and new. And other people, they didn't. Instead of fixin' the church, they built a new one. They asked for donations from the townspeople. Now there's a whole lot of people in Lumberland can't afford that kinda money, but they were willin' to put in their skills and fix this old one. Caused a lot of anger, a lot of meanness. People who put in a lot of money, they don't want the people who didn't comin' to their new church. Now I got a real issue with this. Let me tell you why. I got a real issue with God to begin with, but I don't think prayin' should have anything to do with money. So there's this church in the woods, just rottin' away.

Luke and me, when we came close to the church, we noticed a pickup truck parked outside. Now you can drive to the church from the dirt road, but nobody ever ever comes here anymore. The pickup truck was old and rusty. So Luke and me, we tiptoed real real quiet over to the side of the church, and we peeked through one of the windows. I never been inside the church. Inside there was this altar in the back, this old wooden altar with candles all burned down, and above it, in a sorta alcove, a wooden statue of Christ on the cross. He was all broken, and the wood, where it was painted, was cracked.

With the moon and all startin' to appear, beams of light crisscrossed each other from the stained-glass windows. There were no seats or nothin', just a big empty room. And there was that girl from Domino's, crumpled on the floor, hidin' her face. Her hands were coverin' it, and they were shakin'.

Me and Luke, we snuck around—holdin' our breath so we'd be real quiet—to one of the windows that was broken.

The creepy guy was leanin' over her. He looked like he was gonna explode or somethin'. She took her hands away from her face, and she looked at him like she was beggin'. He grabbed her, and he pushed her up against the wall, hard, real hard, and then he smacked her across the face. The sound reminded me of the first crack of thunder. She held on to her belly with both hands.

"I oughta just leave you here to rot. How'd you like that—just leave you here to rot? Do you some good bein' left."

She didn't say nothin'. Not a word.

I turned to Luke and whispered, "You think she's mute?"

"I think she's scared," he whispered back.

Then the creepy guy started really cursin' at the girl, loud and scary-like. Standin' right over while she curled into a ball in the corner. Just screamin' and cursin'.

Now I know a lot of curse words, and sometimes when I get real angry, I'll say a bad word. Mostly I say 'em to myself. But one time, I said one out loud in front of my dad, and he didn't like it much. I hear him say curse words sometimes. Even says the *F* word. But he don't like me sayin' it. And I hear Jessie curse all the time, when she's talkin' with one of her friends or her sister. But when Jessie and my dad say it, it don't sound mean, just matter-of-fact. This guy sounded mean.

"I wanna leave, Luke," I turned to him and whispered. "I wanna go now." I started runnin', but Luke, he sorta lingered by the window. I hadda turn and whisper loudly, "Come on, Luke, come on."

Luke caught up to me, and we ran and ran and ran until we got to the bridge. We could hardly breathe from all the runnin'. We were holdin' on to our sides, catchin' our breath.

"You think we should call the police or somethin'?"

"I think we should keep our mouths shut, Addie, that guy seems like the type, he found out who tattled on him, he'd get real mean. We go to the police, they're gonna want us pickin' him out. You wanna be the one pickin' him out? Not me."

chapter four

We hardly said a word after that, just walked.

I dropped Luke off at his house. Joyce's car was in the drive. She's got a Toyota. It's got a few bangs in it, some dents. Joyce is always gettin' into some kinda accident. She drives real fast, even when she doesn't have anywhere to go.

"You wanna come for supper, Addie?"

"Uh-huh. I'm just gonna go home first. I'll come on by in about an hour. Is that okay?"

"I'm gonna tell my mom you're comin' over."

"You don't think she made that meatball thing tonight, do you? It upset my stomach the last time, and I don't think my stomach can handle any more upset."

"She only makes that on special occasions. Tonight's just ordinary. See you in an hour."

Luke walked up the path leadin' to his house. I waited

till he got inside, then I walked on home. I couldn't help but think about that girl, havin' that creep's hands, with those bit-down nails, hurtin' her. I just couldn't stop thinkin' about her. Made my skin crawl.

When I got home, Jessie was finishin' up sewin' her dress. It was pink, all right. Bright pink.

"Whaddya think, Addie? Think it's shockin' enough?"

"I guess."

"You guess? Child, it's gonna move more than his heart when I'm wearin' it."

"I'm goin' upstairs, Jessie. I'm gonna take a shower."

"A shower? Why you takin' a shower?"

"I feel dirty."

"You don't look dirty."

"Since when you gotta look dirty to feel dirty?"

I went upstairs and I stripped off all my clothes and I stood under a hot shower. The water just poured down on me. I scrubbed my skin, and when I closed my eyes, all I saw was that girl holdin' her belly.

I musta been in the shower for a long time, 'cause Jessie was poundin' on the door to the bathroom. "What you doin' in there, child? You're usin' up all the hot water. Get out now. Time's up."

I wrapped a towel around me and I opened the bathroom door.

"What's goin' on with you, Addie? It ain't like you to take a shower in the evenin'. What's wrong with you?"

I wanted to tell Jessie about the girl and the creepy guy

hittin' her, but I figured it was best for me to keep my mouth shut. I kept hearin' Luke sayin' "You wanna be the one pickin' him out?"

"Nothin's wrong with me, Jessie. Just wanted a shower, that's all."

She looked at me. Jessie could always tell when I was fibbin'. But this time, I wasn't gonna say nothin'. I went into my room and picked out some new clothes to wear. When I went down to the kitchen, Jessie was takin' a meat loaf out of the oven.

"This is for your lunch tomorrow, you and your daddy. I added some spices, just the way you like it. Tabasco and green peppers." She looked at her watch. "Now your dad wanted to know if you could sleep over Luke's tonight. He's gonna spend the night over at Grayce's. You wanna call up Luke and see if it's okay? 'Cause I don't wanna call there and get that woman on the phone. She'll just slam the phone down on me." Jessie and me, we looked at each other. Like I said earlier, I never said a word to her and she never said a word to me, but I could tell we were both thinkin' the same thing.

I called Luke and asked if I could spend the night there. I hadda hold for a minute while he asked Joyce, then he got back on the phone and said it was okay.

I picked at the meat loaf while it was on the counter. Jessie slapped my hand. "Birds pick at their food, not humans. You wanna pick, go make yourself a nest."

"I wanna ask you somethin', Jessie. Suppose you saw somethin' bad happenin'. What would you do?"

"Depends on what kinda bad you're talkin' about. You see somethin' bad happen?"

"Uh-uh. Just askin'. Would you do somethin' if you did?"

Jessie let out a big sigh, which meant she was gonna try diggin' a little bit. "Why don't you gimme an example of what you're talkin' about. Use your imagination."

"Never mind. I was just askin', that's all."

Jessie gathered her fabric and started gettin' ready to leave. She took her lipstick from her purse and walked over to the mirror by the sink. She rolled the red over her lips, then smacked 'em once, blendin' the color together.

"You ready, Addie? I gotta leave." She put on her coat, picked up her purse, and grabbed her dress, which was hangin' on the door. We walked out of the house together.

"I'm gonna take my bike over to Luke's."

I went behind the house and walked my bike over to where Jessie was standin'.

"I love you, sugar."

"I love you, too, Jessie."

She started to walk toward the sidewalk, then she stopped and turned to me as I was gettin' on my bike. "If I saw somethin' bad happenin', I'm not the type to turn my back. If I saw someone bein' hateful, I'd put my two cents in. I think sometimes walkin' away from evil is just as evil."

I stood there watchin' as she got into her car and pulled away. I just stood there until I couldn't see her car anymore. Then I got on my bike and rode to Luke's. "Walkin' away from evil is just as evil." Huh. I never looked at it that way.

chapter five

Joyce was in a foul mood. Just when I showed up, she was screamin' at Charlie on the phone.

"You keep forgettin', Charlie. Hey, do me a favor, dish that crap out to someone else. You keep forgettin' I know you better than anybody. I went to bed with you, and I woke up with you on and off for twenty-five years, dish your crap out to someone else." She slammed the phone down, then picked it up and slammed it down again and again and again, just poundin' the receiver down on the phone.

"Ass." She turned to Luke and said, "You're dad's an ass. A first-class ass." Then she looked at me. "Hi, Addie, hope you're hungry. I made a big dinner."

Now let me explain a little about Joyce. Joyce and Charlie, they met on a commune, musta been sometime in the seventies. Anyway, that's what Luke says, they met on this commune. Whole buncha people lived there. I think it was in Oregon. Charlie was a musician, played in this rock band, had long hair almost halfway down his back. He played the drums. Joyce was livin' in Oregon, goin' to college there and I think what happened was, and I could be wrong, Charlie's band was playin' like right on the land where the commune was, sorta like an outdoor concert, and Joyce and her friends came, and she never left. She moved in with him, sang in the band for a while. Then she and Charlie they traveled cross-country in a bus or somethin'. Then they broke up.

A coupla years later, they ran into each other. Then they got married, broke up, got back together, broke up, divorced, got back together, and got married again. That's when they had Luke, when they got married again. Joyce wanted to be a singer—"like Joni Mitchell," that's what she used to say. She doesn't talk about singin' anymore. But a lot of the time, when you go over to their house, she's always got music on. She loves music. Sometimes she plays it so loud your ears hurt. She's got long, wavy hair and never ever wears makeup. Ever. And she wears silver jewelry—lots of it.

We sat at the kitchen table. Joyce made some Mexican type of food—tacos and enchiladas. The meat in the tacos tasted just like hamburger. She's always makin' food with chopped meat, like the meatballs that got me sick. The phone rang. Joyce didn't answer it. When Luke got up to get it, she grabbed his arm.

"Don't answer it. Let it ring. Let him worry. It's good for him."

"What if it's not dad?"

"How much you wanna bet? Now sit down and eat. Let it ring."

When Luke sat down at the table, Joyce took her hand and ran it through Luke's hair. Then she smiled at him, all kind and sweet. "I don't mean to yell at you. Just your father gets me . . . He pisses me off."

Joyce turned to me. "You tryin' out for the school play this year, Addie? The one they're puttin' on in December?"

"I don't think so. I don't have much talent singin' or dancin'."

"I love that musical, *West Side Story*. God, what music." She started hummin'. "You know what it's about?"

"I think so. I think me and Luke saw the movie on TV, didn't we, Luke?"

"Yeah, we saw it."

"God, I wanted to be Maria," Joyce said. "Natalie Wood played her in the movie. Did you know that wasn't her real singin' voice? She didn't sing a word; somebody else did. Boy, that's a tragedy, the way she died, on that boat. Did you know that she and Robert Wagner were married and then divorced, and then she married someone else, and then they got back together and remarried?" She turned to Luke and said, "Sorta like your dad and me. Except, of course, they had a lot of money and were famous. We're just sorta makin' ends meet. But there's a similarity. You know who else got married, divorced, remarried?"

Luke and me, we just shook our heads.

"Liz Taylor and Richard Burton. Now the similarity with me and Charlie is that Liz and Dick they used to fight all the time, like cats and dogs."

The phone rang again. This time Joyce answered it. She didn't even say hello, just ripped right in.

"Listen you, don't you call here anymore tonight. I don't wanna hear your voice—" Then there was a brief silent moment. "Oh, hi, Myles. Yeah, she's here. You wanna talk to her? No, it's just Charlie bein' stupid. Here, let me give you Addie."

She pulled the cord so it reached me at the table. "Hey, Dad. Uh-huh. Uh-huh. Nope, I don't wanna. Okay, I will. Okay, I'll see you then. Say hi to Grayce. Uh-huh. Bye. Love you, too." While Joyce was hangin' up the phone, I turned to Luke. "He's goin' over to Hawley tomorrow with Grayce, to the greenhouse. I hate that drive, it's borin'."

"She's a nice woman. I like her." Joyce took the open bottle of wine off the counter and poured herself a nice full glass.

"So, what did you two kids do today, other than make believe you were too sick to go to school?"

Luke and me we looked at each other. I was about to open my mouth when his eyes got real wide, like he was afraid I was gonna say somethin' about that girl and that creep.

"Not much, Mom. Just sorta hung around, played some videos at the Kmart, you know, stuff."

"Did you know Luke's been accepted to go to Princeton next summer to take some special courses?" Joyce said. "He's gonna be gone the whole month of July and part of August. Only a few kids in junior high, in the whole country, get accepted into this program." She took a big gulp of wine, then sorta shook her head. "I'm so proud of you, Luke."

My stomach turned over. It got all tight and everything.

"You're gonna be gone next summer, Luke? I thought we were goin' to camp."

"I was gonna tell you, Addie, but it just happened a few days ago. I got a letter in the mail. Anyway, it's only for six weeks."

Six weeks? That's like forever. My mouth just dropped open. The thought of Luke not bein' here for the summer . . . Who's gonna float with me on the blow-up raft?

"You gonna be gone for July Fourth?"

"Uh-huh."

Well, you coulda just pushed me right off the chair. See, this is what happens when you only got one best friend. When they're gone, who do you got to play with? Now there's a lot of kids my age live around here, and I like some, but when you got a best friend, that's who you spend time with. My dad always says, "Addie, you oughta make other friends. A girl your age should have tons of friends."

I didn't know if I was angry at Luke or disappointed at Luke or sad or anything. I'd never experienced this before, so I didn't know what I was feelin', other than I wanted to cry. Now I wished I had other friends, at least one more. I mean, thinkin' about it right now, at this very moment, I'm gonna have to blow up the raft by myself, bring it down to the river by myself, try and get on it by myself, and then float by myself. Usually Luke blows it up, we carry it together, and then when I get on it, he holds it down for me. Thinkin' about it, know what, I don't even wanna think about it.

"Addie, do you wanna play Monopoly or what?"

"Huh?"

"I asked you twice now. Didn't you hear me?"

"I guess not. Musta been somewhere else, Luke. I don't really feel like playin' Monopoly. Why don't you play by yourself?"

"Can't play by yourself, Addie. You gotta have at least two players."

"Well, now you know how it's gonna be for me next summer."

We didn't play Monopoly. I could hardly even talk to Luke, except to ask him if he was ever gonna tell me about Princeton or was I just gonna wake up one mornin' in July and he was gonna be gone.

"I'm just gonna have to make a new best friend, Luke. I can see I'm not gonna be able to rely on you much longer."

"It's only for six weeks, Addie."

We were sittin' on Luke's roof, lookin' up at the sky. It was real pretty. Tons of stars were out, and Luke was pointin' and tellin' me which star was which. And then eventually he got to the planets.

"Were you ever ever gonna tell me, Luke, huh, ever?"

I was plenty angry. Or maybe I was just feelin' real hurt, which sorta felt like anger.

"I was gonna tell you, Addie, but I feel kinda weird about it. It's not easy bein' so smart, you know."

"I wouldn't know. I got short-term memory. I don't wanna look at the stars anymore. My neck hurts from strainin'. I'm goin' down to the porch."

"Maybe you oughta try lyin' down on the roof, won't hurt your neck so much. The sky looks pretty when you lie down. You almost feel like you're part of the universe."

"You forget, last time I laid down, I slid off the roof. No, thank you. I'm goin' down to the porch."

"Well, I'm stayin'."

"Well, fine."

As I went over to the ladder leanin' up against the house, Luke said, "You're still my best friend, Addie."

When I climbed down the ladder and walked over to the porch, Charlie was sittin' there, right next to the jack-o'-lantern.

I sat down next to him. Charlie wears his hair in a pony-tail. It's all gray, and it comes down to his shoulders. He's always wearin' a pair of jeans and a work shirt. He must have at least ten work shirts, unless of course he's only got one and washes it all the time. But I don't know about that. He's got a nice face, except he has some pockmarks right on both cheeks. Said he had acne when he was a teenager.

"She won't let me in. Maybe if I sit here long enough, she'll relent. Where's Luke?"

"On the roof. Maybe you oughta bring her some flowers. She likes flowers, grows 'em all summer."

"It's gonna take more than flowers. Joyce is a hard nut to crack. How you doin', Addie? You doin' okay?"

"Uh-huh. Did you know that Luke is goin' away this summer?"

"You bet. That son of mine, I tell you, I don't know where he gets it from, but boy, he's somethin'." Then Charlie thought for a minute. "Joyce's dad was a brilliant man, brilliant. When he was a child, he would sit down at the piano and play. Never had a lesson. He just had this gift, was born with it. I think the same is true of Luke. He was born with a gift."

"Why would anyone give science as a gift? I can understand music or paintin', but what kinda gift is science?"

"It's a gift of the mind, Addie."

"Well, I think you oughta give Joyce a gift of flowers—that's a gift of forgiveness."

Charlie laughed, shook his head, and laughed again.

"The Grand Union sells flowers, Charlie, and they're open till midnight."

"You're pretty smart yourself, Addie Goode."

Charlie got into his van, an old VW bus. On the front of

the van, where you would normally have an ornament, well Charlie had taken off the VW ornament and put a peace sign made of metal. It was real cool lookin'. The van was parked right behind Joyce's car. When Charlie drove away, I turned so I could lean against the railin', and I caught Joyce starin' out the window, watchin' the van disappear down the street. She didn't look happy that he had left. She looked kinda sad. I wasn't gonna tell her that he was comin' back with flowers. I thought she could use a surprise.

While I sat on the porch, I had a hundred thoughts goin' through my mind. First Luke, then Charlie and Joyce, which made me think about Jessie, which made me think about what she said about walkin' away from evil is just as evil, which made me think about the girl from Domino's, which made me think about the river, which made me think about the summer. And then I thought, *I gotta get another friend,* which made me think about Luke again and about how bein' a best friend with someone takes so much time and energy. I mean, you don't just become best friends. With me and Luke, it was like we started playin' together and hangin' out together and walkin' to school together and waitin' for each other after school. And then we invited each other over for dinner and lunch and then we would walk somewhere together and then one day, he turned to me and said, "You're my best friend in the whole world, Addie." And I said to him, "You're my best friend in the whole world, too." And then we were best friends.

My head hurts from thinkin' so much. I wished Joyce

coulda waited to tell me about Princeton. I just got too much in my head right now, too much information.

Well, Charlie did come back with about four bouquets of flowers, all mixed, for Joyce. She didn't invite him in, 'cause their date night is Saturday, but they sat on the porch together for a little while, and then Charlie kissed her good night. Me and Luke watched them from his bedroom window, and we saw Charlie give her the tongue.

Luke and me, we musta gone to sleep about one o'clock in the mornin'. We stayed up watchin' TV—some really old, scary horror movie. I slept in a sleepin' bag on the floor. Luke woulda given me his bed, but I like sleepin' in a bag—makes me feel like I'm campin' out. Luke is a real deep sleeper. Nothin' wakes him. He brought in the little night-light from the bathroom so I wouldn't be afraid. Like I said earlier, way earlier, sleepin' in the dark scares me. I don't know why, never figured it out. It just does. I once asked Jessie if she thought there was a reason I was scared of the dark. She said sometimes there are no reasons, but after a while the fear just goes away. "It's like when you have the flu, Addie. You feel like a dog ready to die, then one day you feel better. Some fears are like that."

Anyway, Luke was out as soon as he hit the pillow. I tossed and turned for a while, and then I fell asleep. I had this nightmare. I don't even wanna talk about it. It was hideous, and it woke me up. And the thing I thought about immediately, when I woke up, was that girl in the church. It was like she was right there, in my mind, like I could feel her. I don't wanna talk about the nightmare, but she was in the nightmare. Clear as day. I looked over at the clock on Luke's night table, and it read 6:13 A.M. I was lyin' still for a while, and then I got up, got dressed, folded the sleepin' bag real neat and quiet, and tiptoed out of Luke's room.

I passed Joyce's room, her door was shut. I tiptoed down the stairs, and made sure that I was real quiet, and then I took my sneakers, opened the door, and left.

I sat on the porch, put on my sneakers. The sun was up, all big and bright. Then I went to the side of Luke's house and got my bike.

I rode all the way to the church—you know, the one in the woods. Somethin' told me she was gonna be there. I just felt it inside of me. Now I don't know if you ever had this experience, but there was one part of me sayin', *Addie, mind your own business,* and then there was the other part of me sayin', *Walkin' away from evil is just as evil.* It was like there was a little battle goin' on inside of me. So I stopped ridin' and thought for a moment. Just stood there, surrounded by woods. And then from outta nowhere came five deer, walkin' one after another. I could see them, but they couldn't see me, and there was a fawn tryin' to catch up. I waited till they disappeared in the woods, got back on my bike, and rode to the church.

There was no sign of the pickup truck anywhere. I think if I had seen it, I woulda just kept ridin'. Bein' that it wasn't there, I got off my bike and I walked over to the broken window, to look inside. At first I only saw the altar and the statue of Jesus. But then I strained my neck, and there she was, in the corner of the room. She was on her knees, and her head was bowed.

I opened the door to the church. It was heavy and wooden, an old door. She turned and looked at me, like she was expectin' someone, then she turned away.

"Whatcha doin'?" I asked. She didn't answer, so I asked again, "Whatcha doin'?"

She turned to look at me. "I was prayin'."

"For what, what were you prayin' for?"

She didn't answer me. I walked over to her, stood right next to her, and said, "You look like you could use a meal. You hungry? I bet you're hungry. I bet your baby's hungry. You can come to my house. No one's home, except me, and I can feed you."

She got up off her knees. I looked at her belly; it was so big and round. The side of her face, where she was slapped, was all red and puffy. I could tell she was feelin' ashamed 'cause I was starin' at her. She rubbed her belly with her hand, in a circular motion. "He's kickin'," she said, more to herself than to me. Then she managed a smile. It was sweet and genuine. "There you go again, kickin' away."

"You hungry?" I asked again. She nodded.

I started walkin' out of the church. She was right behind me. I think when you offer people food, it's hard for them to turn you down, especially if they haven't eaten in a while.

We walked through the woods, over the little bridge. I was pushin' my bike the whole way. We didn't say a word. I kept wantin' to say somethin', but I was waitin' for her to say somethin' first. When we got to the road, she looked at me.

"What's your name?" she asked.

"Addie. Addie Goode. What's yours?

"Rachel."

"Hi, Rachel."

"Hi, Addie." And then after a few moments, she said, "I was prayin' for someone to be my friend."

chapter six

"Nice house," Rachel said.

"Uh-huh, we like it. I can make you eggs or pancakes. I can't make French toast, and I definitely cannot make waffles. If Jessie was here, she'd make waffles. But if Jessie was here, then you wouldn't be here, so . . . eggs or pancakes?"

"Eggs sound good. I can make them myself. I know how to cook."

"Well, I invited you here, so you're like a guest, and that means I should cook for you. How do you like 'em, scrambled, over easy . . . ? Those are the two ways I know how to make 'em."

"Scrambled's good."

Rachel sat down at the table. She hadda sorta maneuver herself into the chair, like she was leanin' backward before she could sit.

I took the eggs, butter, and milk out of the fridge. "You want some coffee? I know how to make coffee." She nodded.

"Who's Jessie? Is that your mom?"

"Uh-uh, she's not my mom. Jessie takes care of me and the house and my dad."

"Where's your mom?"

I put some butter in the pan and watched it sizzle. Then I took three eggs, cracked 'em and whipped 'em in a bowl with the milk, and added some salt and pepper. I didn't wanna answer that question, so I just made believe that I was too busy preparin' the breakfast. I decided to make some toast. That's what they do at Dottie and Sy's—they make toast with the eggs and home fries—but no way I was gonna start cuttin' up potatoes. That seemed like too much of a chore. And I made a pot of coffee in the Mr. Coffeemaker.

I brought the plate over to Rachel, placed it on the table, and gave her a napkin and a knife and fork. I sat down in the chair next to her. She had real nice table manners. She placed the napkin on her lap and kept her elbows off the table. And she ate slow.

"You want some milk for your coffee?"

"You have soy milk?"

"What?"

"Soy milk."

"Uh-uh, we don't have that, just plain milk, homogenized. Does that help?"

"I'll drink it black."

I poured her a cup of coffee and put it down in front of her. She looked up at me.

"Thank you very much, Addie."

"You're very welcome, Rachel."

Table manners and graciousness, huh.

I sat down again and I just watched her. Now I woulda been done with that breakfast in about thirty seconds. She musta taken at least fifteen minutes. She would take the corner of the napkin and pat her lips—not like me, just wipin' my mouth with the whole thing. When she finished eatin', she took the plate and washed it. Then put it in the dryin' rack by the sink. There's this itty-bitty photo framed in silver by the sink, on the window ledge. It's of me and my dad when I was about eight years old. He's givin' me a big kiss on my cheek, and I'm smilin' a big smile. Rachel picked it up and held it in her hand.

"This your dad?"

"Uh-huh."

"He's handsome. He has a nice face, a good face."

It's funny how you can look at a picture and sorta see somethin' in it, like the goodness in somebody.

"Where is he now?"

"Right now, this minute?"

"Uh-huh."

"He's at his girlfriend's house. He spent the night." She took another look at the photo, then placed it back on the window ledge.

"How old are you, Addie?"

"Twelve. My birthday's May 7."

"That makes you a Taurus. That's a good sign."

"What sign are you?"

"I'm a Leo. My birthday's August 15. I'll be twenty-four."

Huh. I thought for sure she was younger.

"You're allowed to stay by yourself when he's not here?"

"Uh-huh. I was stayin' over at Luke's house, but I left when I woke up. I'm allowed to be here by myself durin' the day and sometimes at night."

"Was Luke the boy you were with at Kmart?" I nodded. She smiled, she had a nice smile and pretty teeth. Then her face musta been hurtin', 'cause she rubbed the side of her cheek, where it was all bruised.

"You looked at me and smiled," she said. "I thought that was very kind of you."

She started walkin' to the back door, the one that's in the kitchen. "I should be goin'. Thank you again, Addie. You're a very nice person."

"You wanna take a shower or clean yourself up or somethin'? We got a really good shower, it has one of those heads that you can spin and give yourself a massage, you know what I'm talkin' about? Maybe you wanna clean yourself up, it may make you feel better where you've been hurt."

I didn't want her to leave. I don't know why, I just didn't.

She stood there by the door. She looked around the kitchen and sorta took everything in, like she wanted to remember what it looked like. She looked at me. I was just sittin' at the table.

Then the phone rang. I picked it up, and it was Luke. He was wonderin' what happened to me, where I went to. I told him I couldn't sleep, so I came home. He asked me if I wanted to come over for breakfast. I told him I already ate, which was a lie, but how was he gonna know?

"Maybe I'll see you later, Luke." Then I hung up the phone. If I had told Luke that I had gone to the church and now Rachel was over my house, he woulda told me that I was the dumbest person in the world, and I didn't wanna hear that.

"You wanna clean yourself up?"

"I look awful, don't I?"

"Well, to be honest, I don't know what you look like other than what you look like now."

"You sure it's okay for me to shower?"

"Uh-huh, you just gotta make sure you don't stay in the shower for a long, long time. Otherwise, the hot-water heater goes off, and all the water turns cold."

I took her upstairs, showed her the bathroom, and gave her two clean towels—one for her hair and one for her body. The one for her body was a real big one, like a beach towel. It had a design on it—zigzags in all colors.

"There's shampoo and soap and a sponge right on the bathtub."

She closed the door to the bathroom. I stood outside it for a minute, then I went back down to the kitchen. I could hear the water runnin' from the shower. I made myself a bowl of cereal and sat down and ate it, fast. I don't really chew food. I mean, I do, but I don't chew like fifteen times and then swallow. I just eat. My dad always says, "Addie, what's the hurry? Where you goin'? In order to enjoy your food, you need to eat it nice and slow." I enjoy my food fine, thank you. I just enjoy it quicker.

I drank a glass of milk, plain milk. What is soy milk, anyway? I've seen somethin' in the supermarket, Ice Dreams or Nice Dreams or . . . Wait a minute, whatsitcalled . . . A, B, C, D, E, F, G, H, I, J, K, L, M, N, O, P, Q, R—that's it, Rice Dreams. It's right by the Cremora and powdered milk, except it's a liquid. I never drank Cremora, ever. One time, my dad and Luke and me, we went campin', and my dad forgot juice and milk for the mornin', so we pulled into a 7-Eleven, and they didn't have milk, just powdered milk. Gotta add water. It was God-awful. Me and Luke, we spit it right out. Ugh, just thinkin' about it—gotta shake that memory right now. Anyway, wonder if Rice Dreams is the same thing as soy milk. I'll ask Andy. He's a cashier at the Grand Union. He'll tell me.

I was thinkin' about Rachel, up there in the shower. I was tryin' to think what it must be like to be her. If I was her, I'd be scared. I'd be lonely and frightened and scared. I'd be cryin' a lot, probably, cryin' and worried and lonely and scared. But I'd be just as polite as her. She's awfully po-lite. "Polite breeds polite"—that's what Jessie says—which makes me think Rachel musta been raised polite. Then I started thinkin', W*hat if, what if she's a really bad person?* I mean, some bad people are polite, right? Some bad people, when they put a gun to your head, if they're polite, they just may look at you and say, "I'm sorry, but I gotta shoot you." Or if they're holdin' up a bank or somethin', they may say to the teller, "Thank you very much for all that money." You can be polite and bad. What if Rachel was really a bad person? And now she's up in my shower, usin' my water, usin' my soap and shampoo and my towels. I mean, what if what if what if she's a murderer? Oh my God. My hands started tremblin', and my heart started poundin', and my head was gonna explode. The shower stopped runnin'. I looked up at the ceilin', 'cause the bathroom is directly over the kitchen, and I thought to myself, *Addie Goode, when you bring home strays, they got four legs, and the worst thing about 'em is sometimes they got fleas. Now you got a murderer in your bathroom.* I could feel my heart racin'.

"Thank you for the shower. It felt wonderful."

I turned my head, and Rachel was standin' in the doorway, all clean. Her hair was all shiny and wet, and her face was scrubbed. Except for the bruise on her cheek, she was real pretty.

"You ever kill anyone?"

"Excuse me?"

"I said, you ever kill anyone?"

She just shook her head.

"Anyone you know ever kill anyone?"

"I don't think so. Why you askin'?"

I pushed the chair back and stood up. My knees felt real weak, like they were gonna buckle.

"That boyfriend of yours, that creepy guy, he ever kill anyone?"

"I think I better leave now."

She was all clean, but her clothes were old and worn, and they looked worse now. They didn't look right on her anymore. She went over to the door. I just stood there, wishin' she would hurry up and leave. I scared myself to death with all the thoughts I was havin'. Then she turned to me. Her eyes were full, like she was gonna burst.

"I appreciate everything you did for me, givin' me food, lettin' me shower . . ." The tears were streamin' down her face. Her mouth was quiverin'. "It's been a long time since someone's been so nice and kind to me. I forgot what it feels like."

"How long since someone's been nice to you?"

She shrugged. "I don't know—a long, long time."

"What about your mom and dad—don't they love you?"

Then all of a sudden, she just started sobbin'. Sobbin' and sobbin' and sobbin'. I got a Kleenex from the kitchen drawer. Jessie keeps a box of Kleenex next to the sink, for when she's got allergies. I handed it to her. I wasn't sure anymore if I wanted her to leave. I believed she didn't kill anybody. I wasn't sure about that creepy guy, but I really believed she never killed anyone. My mind just sometimes goes into all different places, not all of them good or happy.

"I gotta leave," she said.

"There's some clothes in the barn." Our eyes connected, like for one split second we were lookin' right at each other at the very same time. "They'll fit you. Let me give 'em to you."

chapter seven

Now when I was little, I would go to the barn and I would go upstairs, and I would play make-believe. I would scatter all my dolls on the floor. All of 'em had names. Like for example, I always called Barbie Barbie, but other dolls that didn't already have names, I would name 'em. Like one of my dolls I named after Jessie, except I called her Jessica. I would talk to my dolls and dress 'em, and when one of 'em got sick with a flu or somethin', I would make a little bed for 'em, and tuck 'em in. Only time I ever go up to the barn now is when Luke and me wanna be alone and play. 'Cause usually when we're in the barn, it's 'cause we don't want anyone knowin' what we're doin'. It's sorta like havin' a secret, like on Halloween with the candy.

It's kinda like a storage place, the barn. This is where all the old furniture goes. We got a love seat up there, an old

old old rockin' chair that's broken, a desk, and a few lamps that don't work anymore. Except one. My dad had it in college. It's one of those lava lamps. It's sorta ugly. It's red and has globs of jelly in it, and when you turn it on, the globs of jelly sorta move up and down. At night, when it's the only light on, it looks sorta spooky. Anyway, this is where all the stuff we don't want anymore or don't use anymore gets stored. "One of these days, we're gonna have to go to the Salvation Army, Addie, and get rid of all this stuff, give it to people who can use it." That's what my dad says, but we never do it. It just stays right where it is.

Tucked away upstairs in the back is a bunch of cartons. They've been there for as long as we've lived in this house. They never been opened, except once. Inside those boxes is all the stuff that was my mom's. One time, only one time, I looked in one of them. Me and Luke, we opened the carton, and it was full of clothes, all folded and neat. I got a real funny feelin' when I looked in it. So me and Luke, we just closed it up and that was that.

I pointed to the boxes and I said to Rachel, "Why don't you look through 'em? Maybe you'll find somethin' you can wear."

"Why don't you pick somethin' out for me?"

"I'd rather not."

She sat down on the floor, Indian style. Her belly was like a big mound. She turned to me and said, "You sure about this?" I just nodded and went to sit on the love seat. I decided to sit Indian style, too. It's much easier when you're skinny, and I'm pretty skinny. Sometimes when I suck in my stomach, my ribs pop out. I don't mean like they pop out of my skin, I just mean you can see 'em. One time, me and Luke, we were at the river—this is funny—and there was this couple there. The woman was real chunky, and she was wearin' this two-piece bathin' suit. Now I don't understand why if you're chunky why you would wear a two-piece bathin' suit. I'd wanna hide the fat. Anyway, she was wearin' this two-piece and suckin' in her stomach. Me and Luke, we just laughed and laughed. Her tryin' to suck in her stomach made her look like a balloon.

"This is real pretty," Rachel said, holdin' up a dress with little flowers on it. I looked at it, nodded, then turned my head away. "Whose stuff is this? It looks new."

"It was my mom's."

Rachel placed the dress on her lap. "Did she die?" she asked.

"Maybe."

"Maybe's not a very good answer."

"It's the only one I got. You should just look through the boxes."

Rachel got up off the floor and walked over to me. Uh-oh. I know what this means. It means havin' a conversation. But I figure only way you can have a conversation is if you're both talkin'.

"You don't know if your mom's dead?"

"I don't know a thing about her. Only a little tiny bit."

"Well, where is she?"

"Anybody ever tell you're real nosy?"

Rachel laughed. She's got a good laugh. It's strong and seems like it comes from the gut. Jessie has a laugh like that, too. Whenever she's laughin', it makes me smile. Even if I'm in a bad mood, when Jessie laughs, it's just a real nice sound. I guess I musta smiled. Rachel sat down next to me.

"What's it like carryin' a baby?"

"It's like havin' a bowlin' ball inside you. Except it kicks, and you can feel it move."

"Like a bowlin' ball? I like bowlin'. Me and Luke we go twice a month. They got leagues in Hawley. Hawley's the next town—"

"I know Hawley."

"You do?" She nodded. "Anyway, we go when they have peewee leagues. That means anyone under fourteen gets to bowl, and if you have a good score, over one hundred, you get a trophy. I got two trophies. I know someone who bowled three hundred. That's a perfect game. His name is Paul. He owns the barbershop. He's a real good bowler, goes every week. He's got a big trophy. It's in the window of his shop. You like bein' pregnant?"

"Yeah, I do."

I noticed she wasn't wearin' a wedding band. I didn't notice that before, when she was havin' breakfast. I guess I wasn't payin' much attention to her hands.

"You married?" I asked.

"No, I'm not."

"How come?"

54

"Now who's bein' nosy?"

"Guess we're even."

"Tell you what—I'll tell you why I'm not married if you tell me about your mom."

I needed to think about that. See, the thing is, I never ever talk about my mom. Ever. I never even talked to Luke about her, and he pretty much knows everything about me. I don't even talk to my dad about her, but that's because I know he don't wanna talk about her. Maybe he's talked to Grayce, and I think he's talked to Jessie, 'cause she was the one who told me he's been burned real bad once, so I guess he musta talked to her. Then again, Jessie's got a way of sorta knowin' stuff. I always had this feelin'—I could be wrong—but I always had this feelin' that Jessie sometimes goes through drawers, like a snoop. I think everybody does that. It takes a real strong person to not wanna look through other people's drawers. It's sorta like a magnet, it pulls you to do it. I've done it, gone through my dad's drawers, and one time when I was stayin' over at Grayce's with my dad and they were in the den watchin' TV, I looked in her underwear drawer. It smelled like flowers. Lots of lace and silk underwear. I wear cotton, white cotton. Maybe when I get older, I'll wear lace.

"You first. You tell me why you're not married, then I'll tell you about my mom."

We sat on the love seat, and she told me all about the creepy guy, his name is Trey Sizemore—funny kinda name, don't you think? And she told me that she was livin' with some other guy when she met him, and then she stayed with this other guy—I don't remember his name—and then she and Trey decided to live together. They traveled all over, even to Maine, where he worked at some maple syrup factory, makin' maple syrup which sounds really really icky to me. Then they moved to some other place. To tell you the truth, I was gettin' kinda bored, so I don't remember a whole lot. I just sorta shut my ears and nodded a lot and made believe I was payin' attention when I really wasn't and I started thinkin' about other things.

I musta been really not payin' attention, 'cause she said, "Addie, Addie, Addie . . ."

"Huh?"

"You weren't really listenin', were you?"

"I was, mostly."

She laughed, then she ruffled my hair. She almost looked happy when she laughed.

"Why did he hurt you?" I asked.

"I told him I wanted to get married, bein' pregnant and all. Wanted to give the baby a name—his name." Then she told me that she hadn't seen her mom or dad or talked to them for almost seven years. She said they disowned her, which made me really, really, really sad. The creepy guy wanted her to call them and ask for money, she said, 'cause they have tons and tons of it and 'cause the creepy guy doesn't have a job and, from what it sounds like, is too lazy to go look for one. She told him that she wasn't gonna ask 'em for money and that she wanted to get married, and he got so mad that he hit her. Jessie always says money's the root of all evil. It sure seems like that's true. When I watch the news on TV and they have those stories about someone gettin' murdered over a pair of sneakers or five dollars, I always sit there and think to myself, *Money can make people real mean.*

"That's my story, Addie." I didn't really like that story. I like the ones I make up better.

"You believe in God, Addie?"

"No, I do not."

"Why's that?"

"I got issues with him. Big issues."

"Does it have something to do with your mother?"

"Maybe. How do you know Hawley?"

"I grew up there."

"You did?"

"Yeah, I did. You know Hawley well?"

"Uh-huh."

"You know the fruit stand they have in the summer, right on Ellis Road?" I nodded. I sure did, go there every summer to buy peaches. "Well, if you turn on Ellis Road and go all the way up, there's a house sits on the top of the road—"

"Oh my God, I know that house! Last summer me and Luke took our bikes and we rode up that road. That's the biggest house I ever saw, ever. That's your house?"

"My mom and dad live there."

"It looks like a castle. Me and Luke we snuck around . . . Should I be tellin' you this, 'cause we were trespassin'?"

"You can tell me."

"We looked in the windows. No one was home. I can't believe you grew up there. Wait'll Luke finds out."

Which made me think I should call him. He was probably thinkin' I didn't wanna be his friend anymore. Knowin' Luke, that's definitely what he was thinkin'. See, when you're a best friend with someone, you can tell what's on their mind, sometimes before they do. Even if he wasn't thinkin' at that very moment about why I hadn't called, I bet pretty soon he would be. I should call him. I don't want him thinkin' I don't wanna be his friend.

"It had a lot of pretty things inside. I can't believe it. That's so weird, don't you think, you bein' here, me knowin' your house? You know what Luke always says when somethin' like that happens? 'Course you wouldn't, you don't even know him. He says that's a little piece of magic, you bein' here, me knowin' your house. A little piece of magic."

Rachel grabbed hold of her belly and she sorta turned pale.

"You mind if I lie down, Addie? I'm feelin' so tired."

"You wanna lie down on this love seat?"

"That would be great."

She curled up, and I went to get the blanket that was on the floor. The same blanket I used for Miss Trumbull's pets.

I covered Rachel with it. "It might smell like dogs and cats, but it's clean," I said.

"Thank you, Addie."

"You're welcome, Rachel."

And then she closed her eyes. I sat on the floor and I watched her sleep. And I thought, *She's not a bad person at all. Not at all. Just a lonely heart.*

chapter eight

"Hey, Addie, where are you? Whatcha doin'?"

Luke was standin' outside the barn, yellin' for me. I guess he musta gone to the house and figured maybe I was in here.

I came outside and I musta seemed a little jittery, which I was, bein' that I was sorta hidin' Rachel up in the barn.

"Whatcha doin', Addie?"

"Nothin'."

"Whaddya doin' in the barn?"

Why was everybody bein' so nosy all of a sudden?

"I'm just doin' somethin', that's all. God, can't I do somethin' without bein' questioned about it? I'm busy, Luke, okay?"

"Okay."

We stood there for what felt like forever, but it probably was just a few minutes.

"Maybe I'll see you later, Luke, okay?"

"Okay." Then he said, "It's only six weeks, Addie. I'm only goin' for six weeks."

I figured since Luke thought I was still upset with him, I should just keep it that way. I wasn't really that upset anymore. I mean, I was, but that wasn't why I was bein' jittery.

"I'll talk to you later, Luke. I can't talk now. I'm busy."

He walked away. He reminded me of a puppy with his tail between his legs. One time, I had a puppy in the barn—real small little thing. Anyway, he peed on the floor, and when I came into the barn, he put his tail between his legs. He knew he did somethin' wrong. I look at it this way: Luke shoulda told me he was goin' away for the summer, so maybe it's good he's feelin' bad. Best friends tell each other everything, even things that hurt a bit. I woulda rather him told me than Joyce. Which made me think that maybe I shoulda told him about Rachel. 'Cause you know what's gonna happen? If he finds out, then he's gonna think I kept a secret from him, and then it'll be his turn to be upset with me. And then I'll say somethin' like, "Guess we're even now." Thinkin' about it, I don't like the way that sounds.

"Luke, wait up . . . wait up." I ran over to him. "I'm gonna tell you somethin', but I need you to swear up and down, cross your heart, that if I tell you, you won't say a word to no one. Cross your heart."

Luke, he made a crisscross over his heart.

"You know that girl from the church?" He nodded.

"She's in my barn. Her name's Rachel, and she's real nice and real lonely and real sad."

"What'd you do, Addie? You went there and you got her? That was stupid."

I knew he was gonna say that. I knew it. I thought he was gonna say I was the dumbest person in the world, but sayin' I'm stupid was pretty close.

"I shoulda never told you. Ever. Now I regret it."

"Can I see her?"

"What?"

"Can I see her? Can I look at her?"

"No, you cannot see her, Luke. She's not a pet. Besides, you think I'm stupid. I shoulda never told you. Only reason I told you was 'cause I don't like keepin' secrets from you, even though you like keepin' secrets from me."

Luke and me, we just stood there. He was starin' down at the grass, and I was starin' down at the grass, and we just sorta stood there.

"I don't like fightin' with you, Addie."

"I don't like fightin' with you, Luke."

Then we both looked at each other, and I patted him on the back.

"You wanna see her?"

"Uh-huh."

"Okay, then, but she's sleepin', so we gotta be real quiet, okay?"

"Uh-huh."

I took him up to the barn, and we tiptoed upstairs.

Rachel was all curled up on the love seat. Me and Luke we stood there, just lookin' at her.

"She's pretty," Luke whispered. I nodded. "How old is she?"

"Almost twenty-four. She's a Leo. You know anything about that?" I whispered back.

Luke nodded. I tiptoed away from the love seat and waved to him to come with me. We went downstairs.

"Whaddya know about Leos?"

"It's the Lion, that's what the sign is. Leo the Lion."

"What sign are you?"

"Sagittarius the Archer."

"What's a Taurus?"

"It's the stupid sign, Addie." Luke was jokin', 'cause he laughed when he said it.

"I don't wanna talk about this anymore, Luke."

"You gonna keep her here in your barn?"

"I don't know what I'm gonna do. I fed her and I let her take a shower, and now she's sleepin'. You know where she's from, Luke? She's from Hawley. You know that gigantic house on Ellis Road, the one we went to last summer? That's her family's. She don't talk to them anymore."

"Why's that?"

"Why's what?"

"Why doesn't she talk to them anymore?"

"I think it's 'cause she moved in with some guy and they disowned her."

"The creepy guy?"

"Uh-uh, not him. I can't tell you the whole story right now. It's too long and really borin', and I don't remember all of it. Anyway, I haven't made up my mind what I'm gonna do. Maybe I'll let her stay till tomorrow or somethin'."

"You gonna tell your dad?"

"Now would I have told you a secret and made you cross your heart if I was gonna blab this to everyone? I'm not tellin' my dad."

"What if he finds out?"

"Findin' out is different than tellin'."

"You wanna go for a bike ride?"

"I don't know if I should leave her alone; besides, my dad's gonna be home around three. What time is it now?"

Luke looked at his watch. He's got one of those Casio watches. It glows in the dark and can tell time all over the world, like in Australia or Germany or Colorado. "It's almost nine-thirty."

Nine-thirty? It felt like a whole day had gone by already.

"Huh. Well, I guess that means he won't be home for almost six hours. Maybe I can leave her alone. You think I should?"

"I think if you do, you should lock your house."

We never lock our house. Well, that's not true, a hundred percent. Sometimes we do, like when me and my dad go away for a while. Like when we go visit my grandma and grandpa, they live in Florida, in a town—I forget what it's called. Wait a minute—A, B, C, D, E, F, G, H, I, J, K, L, M, N, O, P, Q, R, S, T—Tamarac. It's all the same houses one after another. One time, me and my dad, we went out to the Friendly's to get ice cream, and when we came back, we didn't know which house was theirs. Every house is exactly the same, and at night they're more the same. We drove around, then we started all over again. My grandma, she was standin' outside her house, hands on her hips, and when we got outta the car, she said, "Myles, where were you? You said twenty minutes. We were worried." Good thing she was standin' outside. Anyway, we locked our house then. We were gone for a week, and Jessie, she took that week off. I don't know where Jessie went that week, all I know is that she broke up with her boyfriend. She wasn't too upset, reason I know this, she sewed a whole buncha party dresses.

Now I was thinkin', if I locked the house and my dad came home and found the door locked, that'd make him curious. And then he'd ask me, "Why'd you lock the door, Addie?" Then I'd have to lie and say, "I don't know, guess I just did." Then he'd know that I was lyin'—he has a way of knowin' that—and that'd make everything worse. But if I don't lock the door, what if, what if, what if Rachel's a snoop? What if she decides that she wants a look through the house, the drawers, our personal things? Like I said, it takes a strong person not to snoop.

I decided to lock the house. I went up to the barn and I very gently woke up Rachel. "Sorry to bother you, but me and Luke, we're goin' for a bike ride. You can stay—just stay here in the barn. Is that okay with you?"

"Yes. Thank you. I'll stay right here and try and sleep."

"Okay, then, you want anything from town? Like ice cream or pickles?"

"No, thank you. I'm fine, Addie, just fine. Not all pregnant women like ice cream and pickles."

"I don't know many. Actually, I don't know any. I just seen that on TV once. Okay, then, I'll see you later."

Me and Luke, we made sure all the windows and all the doors were locked from the inside. I took the key that was hangin' on a hook in the kitchen and locked the kitchen door from the outside.

We walked my bike over to Luke's house. Joyce was sittin' on the porch, her face was all red and blotchy. "Your dad's had a heart attack, Luke, early this mornin' at the bar," she said.

Me and Luke we just almost fainted. Luke started cryin', and I started cryin' 'cause Luke was cryin' and 'cause I really, really like Charlie. Charlie sometimes bartends at Pete's. That way, he can make some extra money and have free drinks, like killin' two birds with one stone.

On Fridays and Saturdays, except when he has a date with Joyce, he works there from 10:00 P.M. to 5:00 A.M. On weekends, the bar stays open till mornin'. My dad says you can go in on a Friday and come out on Sunday.

"Is he dead, Mom, is he dead?"

"No. But he's in the hospital. Your dad's one lucky man. I'm gonna go to the hospital. You wanna go?"

"I wanna go with you, Joyce. I wanna see Charlie," I said.

"I wanna go, Mom," Luke said.

Joyce just sat there, like she couldn't move. Me and Luke we sat down next to her, me on one side and Luke on the other.

"Is he gonna be okay, Mom, is he gonna be okay?"

"He better be."

Then Luke did somethin' I never seen him do before. He took Joyce's hand and he held it. I looked over at him and I smiled, and I thought to myself, *Boys are okay—sometimes.*

chapter nine

Me and Luke and Joyce, we went to Trinity Hospital. It's old and gives me the creeps. I hate hospitals. Hate 'em. One time, my grandpa, he got sick, this was before he and my grandma moved to Florida. He had some kinda ministroke. His mouth drooped down, and he could barely speak a word. Anyway, me and my dad we went to visit him, and boy, did that place smell bad. It smelled like really bad mouthwash. I was too young to go into my grandpa's room. I hadda stay in the waitin' area—a whole buncha people and me just sittin' waitin'. They had a TV attached to the ceilin', and all it played was the news. Between the smell of the hospital and the news, I couldn't have been more unhappy. Trinity Hospital smells just as bad. Since I wasn't immediate family, I couldn't go in to see Charlie right away. First it hadda be Luke and Joyce. But I told Luke and Joyce to say hi for me.

I walked around the hospital for a while. Sick people everywhere: in wheelchairs, usin' canes, old people, young people, lots of people pacin' back and forth, back and forth. Lots of doctors and nurses walkin' around. I bought a soda and pretzels in the vendin' machine. A coupla times, I got asked, "Are you lost?" or "Where you goin'?" or "Are you visitin' someone?" Every time I said, "I'm okay."

I went into the waitin' room. There was a whole family sittin' there—a mom and a dad and three kids. The mom looked like she'd been cryin' for days. The dad had his arm around her. One of the kids looked at me and smiled. I smiled back. I was tryin' to figure out why they were there. I didn't think askin' was the right thing to do. I mean, you don't just go up to someone and say, "Excuse me, how come you're in the hospital?" So I tried figurin' out what was wrong. What I came up with was, one of their other kids musta got in a horrible accident. A car accident. A whole carful of kids, and the driver was speedin'. Goin' much faster than he shoulda, and the car spun outta control and flipped over, then flipped over again, and everyone went through the windshield, and there was blood all over the place. And now they're waitin', 'cause their kid completely disfigured his face and now he needs his whole face done over, and when the doctor's done with him, he's not gonna look like anyone in his family anymore.

The doctor came into the waitin' room. "Mrs. Deer-field . . ."

The woman stood up and said, "Yes?"

Then he said that her mother, she was gonna be just fine and that they were gonna keep her in the hospital for a few days.

She said, "Thank you."

Boy, did I feel stupid. Then I thought, *Maybe, maybe, maybe her mother got in a car accident. That's possible.*

"Excuse me, what's wrong with your mother?" I hadda know, even though it was none of my business.

"Her gallbladder."

"I hope she's okay."

"Thank you. That's very nice."

"You're welcome."

I liked my story better.

Then they left, the whole family, and I just sat there by myself. There was a stack of magazines on the table—all health magazines. Those aren't even good to look at for pictures.

So, I just sat. And sat, and sat. Then I got to thinkin' about Charlie and Joyce and how scary it must be when somethin' happens to somebody that you love a whole lot. Even though Charlie and Joyce sometimes act like they don't like each other, they do. I once heard Jessie sayin' on the phone to her sister, "If I didn't love you so much, Darnelle, I couldn't hate you this much." That's what she said. It's gotta be real scary.

Like the time I had measles. I had the worst case ever. I was covered from head to toe with measles. They were everywhere. And one night, I got so sick 'cause the measles they were all over my face and they got into my ears and I couldn't hear. I could hear a little bit, but that was it, just a little bit, and my dad he was so scared. He came into my room and he crawled in bed with me, and he held me with all his might. What I did hear was how much he loved me and didn't want anything to happen to me. Which made me think if anything ever, ever, ever happened to my dad, I don't know what I'd do. I bet right now, at this very minute, Joyce is sittin' there, lookin' at Charlie, and thinkin', even if she wasn't sayin' it, she was glad that nothin' too awful happened. And knowin' Joyce, she's probably thinkin' it, not sayin' it.

A man walked into the waitin' room. He was way older than my dad, hadda be about seventy. He was dressed nice, had on a nice sweater and a nice pair of gray pants. And he had on a pair of really nice shoes. I like shoes—always look at people's feet to see what they're wearin'. When I get older, I'm gonna have a closetful of shoes. Anyway, he sat down on the couch across from me. He seemed awfully sad. He picked up a magazine and didn't read it, just looked through it. Then he picked up another one and did the same thing. Then he looked at his watch, got up from the couch, and walked back and forth, real nervous-like. I just kept watchin' him. I figured if he looked at me, I'd say, "You okay?" which would maybe get him to talk to me. But he didn't look at me. I was gonna try and figure out why he was in the waitin' room, but it's easier when a whole family's there. When it's only one person, it could be anybody in the hospital.

Luke came in and waved to me. "You wanna see my dad now? He can see you."

"He can see me?"

"Uh-huh. Said so himself."

I got up off the chair, and as I was passing this man, I stopped and looked at him. "I hope whoever you're waitin' for, mister, is gonna be okay."

He looked right at me and just nodded. I nodded back.

When Luke and me left the waitin' room, I asked him how Charlie was doin'.

"He looks like he's ready to beam up."

"How's your mom?"

"Doin' better now."

I got a little jittery goin' into the hospital room, and when I saw Charlie lyin' there, with all these round things stuck on him and a machine connected to his heart, he really did look like he was gonna beam up.

"Hey, Addie, see that? Buyin' her flowers gave me a heart attack."

"It wasn't the flowers, Charlie. It was that kiss you gave her on the porch."

Joyce looked at me and Luke. "You two, nothin's a secret with you two."

"We got plenty of secrets, Joyce," I said. "It's just you don't have any from us."

Luke and me, we got a deck of cards and played on the floor. Joyce sat in a chair right next to Charlie. She held his hand. I never seen Charlie sick before, only with a cold or somethin'. He looked smaller lyin' down. The nurse came in with a tray of food that looked worse than school lunch. Charlie just pushed the tray away when the nurse left, and he asked Joyce to bring him somethin' decent when she came back later.

"What, like a steak with all the fat on it? Charlie, you're goin' on a diet the minute you walk outta here. If you think this food is crap, wait'll you see what I'm gonna be servin' you."

"Does that mean you're lettin' me come home, Joyce?"

"We'll burn that bridge when we come to it."

"I guess that's a yes, Joyce."

chapter ten

Me and Luke, we walked home from the hospital—not a walk I would recommend to anyone who's got problems with their feet. You gotta go up a big hill. Goin' down isn't bad; it's the goin'-up part. You start breathin' real heavy just when you reach the top. I always have to sit down. So, me and Luke, we sat down. We counted four cars passin'. That's it, just four. Charlie hadda have some tests done, and Joyce didn't think we should watch. I didn't wanna stay at the hospital, and Luke didn't either. So we just left. Now, me and Luke, we were just sittin', and Luke seemed too quiet. Didn't say a word to me the whole walk. Sometimes when you're walkin', you don't wanna talk. Even me. But now that we were just sittin' and we weren't sayin' anything, I was beginnin' to get bored. Luke looked like he was thinkin' about somethin', and when Luke's lookin' that way, sometimes you just gotta tap him on the arm.

"Whatcha thinkin' about, Luke?"

"I'm thinkin' about what woulda happened if my dad died."

"What woulda happened?"

"I don't know, bein' that he's not around every day, I don't see him that much anyhow. But I just wonder, what if I never saw him again?"

"I'd be very sad, Luke. I like Charlie." Then I got to thinkin', but sometimes when I'm thinkin', it's out loud. "Wanna ask you, Luke, I don't mean to be freaky about this, but what if, what if, I mean, since you don't believe in heaven or hell after you die, where do you think Charlie woulda gone if he'd died?"

I think Luke sorta liked that I asked that, 'cause he smiled at me. "I think he'd be somewhere in the middle, Addie."

I nodded, and he nodded. But then it got me thinkin' about never seein' Charlie again, which got me thinkin' about what would happen if I never saw my dad again, which got me thinkin' about my mom, who I never, ever think about, mostly 'cause I hardly knew her. I don't even remember what she looked like. One time when I was about five, I was in bed and it was late and I was thinkin' about her, and I was thinkin' about her 'cause my dad was talkin' on the phone to someone about her, and I overheard him. So I closed my eyes and I tried to force myself to see her face—you know, like when you squeeze your eyes closed and try to remember somethin'—but I couldn't. There was nothin' there. Just a lot of nothin'. If somethin' happened to my dad, I wouldn't even have to try and remember what he looked like. I would just know.

Then I started thinkin' about Luke goin' away for six weeks, and I guess I started to cry, 'cause Luke looked at me and said, "What's the matter, Addie?" But I didn't feel like tellin' him I was gonna miss him an awful lot, so I just said that it made me sad thinkin' about maybe Charlie dyin'.

"You don't have to be sad, 'cause he's not dead."

"I know, Luke, but just thinkin' about it . . ."

Then Luke put his arm around me, and we just sat. His puttin' his arm around me made me start missin' him more.

When we got down the hill, Miss Sinclair was takin' groceries out of her car. She doesn't let anyone call her by her first name, Ramona, she doesn't like anyone callin' her that. It's always Miss Sinclair. Anyway, she's sorta friends with Jessie. I mean, they're not good good friends. Jessie says they're "friendly acquaintances." Miss Sinclair is always in a bad mood. Even when she's in a good mood, she's nasty. And I bet if you saw her, you'd think she was maybe fifty or somethin'. But you know what? She's younger than Jessie. She just looks old—old and mean. And she's got this big old house—a Victorian—and it's painted purple and green. Luke calls it the vomit house.

"Hey, Miss Sinclair," I said. Me and Luke stood by her

picket fence. She kicked the door to her car closed and turned and looked at us.

"Addie Goode, what you doin' around here?"

"Me and Luke, we were at Trinity Hospital, his dad had a heart attack, but he's fine now."

"Charles had a heart attack, Lucas? Is that right?"

"It's Luke, not Lucas. I hate bein' called Lucas. And my father's just fine, thank you." Then under his breath, he said, "Ramona." I think she heard him, 'cause her eyes got like slits, and then she turned and walked away from us.

"Bye, Miss Sinclair," I called.

Now I know somethin' about Miss Sinclair that she doesn't know that I know, and I know this 'cause I was eavesdroppin' on my dad talkin' to her one day. She used to live with another girl, another woman named Freda, and they're lesbians. Anyway, Freda left her and moved in with another woman who lives in Philadelphia. And I gotta tell you, I didn't know Freda, except when I saw her in town, but she was a lot nicer than Miss Sinclair. Least she smiled when she saw you. And she always said hello first. And now Miss Sinclair, she's suin' Freda for somethin' called galimony. Now after I overheard the conversation, I needed to find out what galimony was, 'cause I never heard that word before and I was gonna ask my dad, since he's suin' Freda for Miss Sinclair, but my dad he doesn't like eavesdroppers. So I asked Jessie, and she told me that when two people live together and they're not married, they can sue each other for money. And that's called palimony, and bein' that this is two girls, it's called galimony. I don't get it. I don't get why when you live with someone and it doesn't work, why you just can't leave and just not talk to that person anymore. Especially if you're movin' so far away, like Philadelphia, and you don't ever, ever have to see that person again.

"Did you know that Miss Sinclair's a lesbian, Luke?"

"Uh-huh. You told me."

"I did? How come I don't remember?"

"Short-term memory. Mary Castle's a lesbian, too."

"I did not know that. She's real pretty. She wears nice shoes. How do you know that?"

"My mom told me."

"You think she's friends with Miss Sinclair?"

"I don't think Miss Sinclair's got friends. She's too mean."

"You gonna come over later, Luke?"

"Maybe. I hate when she calls me Lucas."

I could tell Luke was in a bad mood now. Miss Sinclair can do that to you. I guess that's what happens when you're mean: you put everyone else in a mean mood. No wonder she don't have hardly any friends.

chapter eleven

Luke wanted to go straight home and read somethin'. I don't know what he wanted to read, but it was probably definitely somethin' I would never read, so I just walked him home.

"So you wanna have supper with us tonight, me and my dad?"

"Whaddya havin'?"

"I don't know, maybe pizza, probably pizza."

"From Tony's?"

"I guess."

"Yeah, sure."

"I'll see you later, Luke. Have fun readin'."

The minute I got home, I unlocked all the windows and doors. My dad wasn't home yet, so it seemed like the right thing to do, otherwise, like I said, he'd get real curious about me lockin' everything, and I wasn't in the mood for that kinda curiosity. Then I walked straight to the barn. Now let me just explain somethin'. You can see the barn from our house, but it's way back toward the woods. I mean, even though you can see it, it's a good full-minute walk. Me and Luke, one day last summer, we counted it—one Mississippi, two Mississippi. When we got to sixty, we were at the barn. One full minute.

In the spring and the summer, the whole area between our house and the barn is covered with wildflowers, all sorts. We got daffodils and daisies and crocuses and what's it called? A, B, C, D, E, F, G, H, I, J, K, L—lilies, lots of lilies. Jessie, she'll come out with scissors and she just cuts all the flowers and then the whole house, in every room—well, that's not true, not every room, but almost—has flowers. Jessie loves flowers, sometimes she'll even put a flower behind her ear. She says that Billy Holiday—she was a jazz singer; I don't know if that's how you spell her name, 'cause that's how you spell it for a boy, maybe it's not spelled like that—anyway, she used to put a flower in her hair. But I don't remember the kinda flower, and in this particular case, goin' through the alphabet wouldn't help me.

Anyway, when I was walkin' to the barn, it just made me think about how pretty everything looks in the spring.

When I got to the barn, Rachel wasn't there. The blanket was on the love seat, and some of the boxes were open, and there was stuff, like letters and pictures, on the floor. But she wasn't anywhere, and I got sad. I just expected she would be there and she wasn't, and I didn't feel like puttin' the stuff back in the boxes, 'cause I didn't feel like seein' what any of it was. Then I got to thinkin' that Rachel was a snoop, and on top of that a messy one.

"Anyone doesn't clean up after themselves don't deserve havin' much." That's what Jessie always says. She always says it to me when my room is messy, which is pretty regular. "Looks like a tornado hit," Jessie says. But then I thought she didn't know which boxes had clothes in them, so I stopped bein' so upset about the boxes. But still, I didn't feel like puttin' everything away, it wasn't my mess, and I got enough problems with my own messes, let alone someone else's. Then I started to wonder, *What if I never saw Rachel again? What if she left?* And I started to feel sad, 'cause I was beginnin' to think of her as a new friend, and how I was probably in need of some friends 'cause of the Luke situation. Sometimes I wonder, *How come one thought in your head triggers a whole other one?* No wonder people get headaches.

"Hi, Addie." Rachel was walkin' up the steps, and she was wearin' this big blue sweater with pockets.

"I hadda pee real bad, so I went into the woods."

"I thought you were gone. If you gotta go to the bathroom, there's a little push door over there, right in the corner of the barn. It looks like a shutter, but it's a little bathroom. It was here when we moved here. I guess maybe someone was gonna make this a room one time but never

81

did. If I was gonna make this a room, I would add a shower. So if you need the bathroom, it's over there. I probably shoulda told you. I just don't think about people peein' a whole lot."

Then she got back on the love seat and curled up in a ball.

"I'm not feeling very good. Maybe I'm comin' down with somethin', maybe a cold." She looked kinda funny, pale and droopy. Like when I was sick with the flu, I looked like that.

"Maybe you need to eat. You feel like eatin'? Jessie made this meat loaf, and she's a real good cook, maybe that'll make you feel better."

"Maybe. Maybe I'm just hungry."

"Okay, I'll be right back. You want somethin' to drink?"

"Water's good."

"Okay, I'll get you some water."

"Come here, Addie, come here. You gotta feel him." She seemed all excited. I went over to her, and she took my hand and placed it on her belly. And the baby, the baby was kickin' and movin' and dancin' around.

"Wow! I can feel him, Rachel, I can feel him. You think it's a him or a her?"

"I don't know. I just always say him. It's like a habit."

It was such an unbelievable thing, feelin' that baby movin'. It was like he was kickin' to get out. Then he stopped, like he was goin' back to sleep or somethin'. It made me giggle.

I was puttin' the meat loaf on a plate when the phone

rang. It was my dad, and he sounded a little upset, 'cause he tried callin' and I wasn't home and then he tried callin' over at Joyce's and nobody was home there. I told him about Charlie and him havin' a heart attack and everything. My dad really likes Charlie, thinks he's funny, and I could tell on the phone that my dad was upset with the news. "He's gonna be okay, Dad. And you know what? Joyce's takin' him home, and she's gonna take care of him, so I guess he's gonna be home now." Then I could tell my dad was tellin' Grayce what was goin' on, and I could hear her sayin', "Is he okay, Myles? Is everything okay?" and he was sayin', "Yeah, I think. Addie said he was okay." And I just wanted to get off the phone, 'cause there's somethin' really annoyin' when you're on the phone and the other person is talkin' to someone else while all you're doin' is keepin' the phone up to your ear.

"Dad, can I go now? I'm sorta busy with somethin', and you can talk to Grayce by yourself, okay?"

Then he said he would be home in about an hour.

"Can we have pizza tonight, Dad? 'Cause I invited Luke and I told him we were havin' pizza and Luke really likes pizza, so can we?"

Pizza sounded good to him. That way, nobody had to cook, and that means nobody had to do dishes. And when Jessie's not around, I usually have to do the dishes, and I hate that. I always break somethin', always. Last time I did the dishes, I broke a glass. I think what happens, your hands are all wet and slippery, and then it's easy for somethin' to break. It's a good thing that it's mostly just me and my dad eatin', 'cause we used to have six plates, but now we only have four, which is okay when we have company like Luke or Grayce, but more than four, we gotta use paper plates.

My dad told me he loved me, and I told him I loved him back, and then we said goodbye. He always, always says he loves me before we say goodbye on the phone. One time, he forgot to tell me, and he called me right back. Jessie always says you should never go to bed angry at someone and you should always tell 'em you love 'em. "Love makes your heart grow bigger and stronger." That's what she says. Maybe Charlie had a heart attack 'cause of the problems between Joyce and him. Maybe his heart shrunk up a bit. Thinkin' about that, I bet that's what musta happened.

Rachel didn't hardly eat anything. She just sorta pushed the meat loaf around. I know she had a coupla bites, 'cause she said she liked the way it tasted. Jessie knows how to cook good. Sometimes she forgets and adds too much stuff, like spices, and I don't really like hot, hot food. One time, I burned the top of my mouth, and for about three days, I couldn't taste anything. Now I tell her, "Jessie, don't make it so hot." Then, of course, she waits for me to say please.

Rachel wasn't lyin' down and she wasn't sittin' up; she was just sorta half-and-half. And she looked really sick, like maybe she had a fever.

"You have your period yet, Addie?"

"Uh-uh. Not yet, but I'm gettin' titties. They're real small, and I can tell they're growin'. I put Band-Aids on 'em. Jessie has a feelin' that I'm gonna get my period when I'm thirteen. That's her guess."

"That's when I got mine."

"Did you like gettin' it?"

"No. I get awful cramps. I can curl up in a ball for two days. I heard that after I have my baby, my periods aren't gonna hurt anymore. You ever kiss a boy?"

"Uh-uh. Ick." The thought of kissin' a boy . . . Ick. "I kissed Luke, but it was a friendly kiss, not on the mouth, if that's what you mean. When's the first time you kissed a boy?"

"First time I was your age, twelve. But when I was fifteen, that was a real good kiss. His name was Danny, lived over in Layton. He was the best-lookin' boy I ever saw. He was tall and had long, dark hair and the prettiest green eyes. He kissed good."

"What's a good kiss like?"

"Well, for starters, it's not sloppy. Sometimes boys like to kiss real wet and sloppy. They put their whole mouth on yours, and they sorta suck on your lips like they're eatin' an orange. Those aren't good kisses. The good ones are slow and dry, and then they get a little wet. When you get older, you'll know the difference."

"Jessie told me once—she made me laugh—she said she had a date with a guy, he kissed her so hard, he bit into her lip. Jessie's so funny, the way she told it, she kept bitin' down on her lip to show me how he did it. She had a big bruise right by her chin."

"You miss not havin' a mom, Addie?"

"Uh-uh. I don't really know what it's like havin' one. Besides, I got Jessie and I got my dad. I got enough. You ever miss your mom?"

"Yeah. I miss her now that I'm gonna have a baby. Makes me think about her a lot. And I really miss my dad. I was his little girl. He used to always call me his little princess. When I was small, every Sunday he and I would have our time, just us. He would take me out to breakfast and then we'd go drivin', and sometimes we'd go to a movie or a museum." She got real sad, her eyes filled up, and she was sorta quiet for a minute. "I think there's a bond between fathers and daughters that goes real deep. I don't know why, I just think that."

"I know what you mean. I wanna ask you somethin', and you don't have to answer, but I'm gonna ask anyway. You gonna keep your baby?"

"Of course. Why you askin'?"

"'Cause some people, some people don't. Some people leave their babies. I mean, even two or three years old is still a baby. Some people do that."

"Well, I won't. I can promise you that."

"You oughta not promise that to me. You oughta promise that to your baby." Me and Rachel looked at each other at the exact same moment. I knew she knew what I was thinkin', so I didn't feel like I hadda say anything more on that subject.

"My dad's gonna come home soon, so this is what I'm thinkin'. You can stay here in the barn, bein' that you're not feelin' good. But if he finds out that I let you stay here, he's gonna have a canary, so I'd really like it if you could stay here and be quiet. And I'll come and visit you every chance I can, like right after dinner and before bed. Is that okay with you?"

"That's good with me. I'm just gonna try and get some sleep."

I was walkin' out of the barn when Rachel called out to me. "You oughta ask Jessie to get you a training bra. It'll feel a lot better than Band-Aids."

"A training bra?"

"It's a little stretchy bra. It'll even help them grow. That's why it's called training—to train 'em. You can probably get one at the Kmart."

"They come in colors?"

"Yeah."

"Good, 'cause I like pink."

Just when I was about to walk down the stairs, I turned to her and I pointed over to the boxes. "You think when you feel better you can put all that stuff away?" And then I said, "Please?"

chapter twelve

"Addie Goode, I'm ashamed of you."

My dad stood right by my bedroom door. I just covered myself with all my blankets and didn't say a word to him. Reason he was ashamed of me, he told me he was gonna marry Grayce. Said he asked her that afternoon.

Now two things were goin' through my mind. They were sorta swirlin' around. First thing, I had no idea that my dad wanted to get married to Grayce. I knew he liked her and all, but gettin' married means you really love someone, and I had no idea he really, really loved her. That's the sorta thing you would know about. I just sorta thought he would tell me. You know, like, "Addie, guess what? I love Grayce. I really, really love her." But he never said that to me, ever. So I just stuck to him likin' her and left it at that. Second thing, and it sorta came outta somethin' he said:

"It's time you had a mother, Addie. All girls need a mother."

I didn't need a mother. I didn't want a mother. I already had one, and it didn't work out. So I blurted out real loud and angry, "I don't want Grayce to be my mother." Now Grayce was sittin' in the livin' room when I said that, and I could tell my dad was embarrassed and everything. Normally, I try and not hurt him, but this time I couldn't help myself. I stormed upstairs and went into my room. I didn't close the door or nothin', so I could hear them talkin' downstairs. It's not really eavesdroppin' when you don't close the door. It's just overhearin', that's all.

"It's okay, Myles. I think I should go home. You oughta be with Addie."

"It's not okay, Grayce. Addie needs to have better manners, and I don't want you leaving."

Better manners? I say please. I say thank you. Maybe not all the time, but most of the time.

"I'm so ashamed of you. You hurt Grayce, and you hurt me, and that's not like you." He just stood there, lookin' at me.

"I don't understand. We're doin' okay. We're doin' just fine—you, me, and Jessie. If I got any girl issues, I talk to Jessie. Grayce can be your wife, but she can't be my mother. I don't want one."

"I thought you liked her."

"I like her. I like her plenty. Why can't I just like her?"

"I want you to apologize, Addie. I want you to call her and apologize."

"Uh-uh. Why should I say I'm sorry if I'm not? You always tell me don't say you're sorry if you think you're right. Well, I think I'm right."

"You're bein' very stubborn, Addie."

"I am not bein' stubborn. How can you teach me somethin' and then tell me that I should be sorry about somethin' I'm not sorry about?" Which made me think about the time in school I had this girl in my class, Melissa. She was real mean, and she made fun of everyone. She called this one girl, her name is Prancer—her mother named her after one of the reindeer—"four-eyes fat tubby Dumbo," that's what Melissa called her. "Four-eyes fat tubby Dumbo." Now Prancer was pretty chunky, I gotta admit. Anyway, one day after school, this girl Melissa, she followed Prancer into the schoolyard, and she kept callin' after her, "Dumbo, Dumbo, Dumbo, Dumbo," and Prancer, she just cried. She sat on the bleachers and she just cried. You know the kinda cryin' when snot comes outta your nose and you can barely breathe? That's the kinda cryin' she was doin'. I went right up to Melissa, and I told her that she was Satan. I just looked her in the eye and said, "You're so mean, you're probably Satan." She told me I hadda apologize to her for sayin' that. I told her I wouldn't, that she oughta apologize to Prancer. She told me she would never apologize to her. Then she said I better apologize to her, Melissa, and I said uh-uh, no way. And she said, "You're not even friends with her." And I said, "So what?" Anyway, point is, when I got home, my dad and me we were talkin', and I told him all about Melissa and Prancer. And you know what he said? He said, "Don't you apologize to her, Addie. That's called standing up for yourself."

Well, that's what I'm doin' now. I'm standin' up for myself.

"Can you please leave me alone, Dad? I just wanna be alone."

I heard my dad walkin' down the stairs, and I thought to myself, *Too much stuff is happenin' this weekend.* Normally, things are pretty quiet around here; things are simple. Now I had issues I hadda deal with, that were hittin' me all at once: Rachel, Grayce, Charlie, Luke goin' to Princeton. It was like, all of a sudden, I was in the middle of a hurricane. Then I remembered somethin' Jessie said. She said sometimes everything happens at once. Like the time her boyfriend left her and her house got robbed and her dog got sick and her sister had a baby. Happened all at once. "I call it one full swoop, child, one full swoop." Well, I'm havin' a one-full-swoop kinda weekend.

I stayed in my room, in my bed. I wondered if my dad had bought Grayce a ring and everything. Wondered if he got down on his knee and said, "Grayce, will you marry me?" Wondered if the reason they were gettin' married was 'cause maybe she wants a have a baby. Jessie always says that women have this clock that ticks inside them and I'm not real sure about this, but I think when they're ready to have a baby, the alarm goes off. Maybe Grayce's alarm went off. Maybe that's what happened. Maybe she and my dad were talkin' one day and her alarm went off and she said, "Wanna have a baby, Myles?" I don't know why I'm so upset, but I'm so upset I could scream. I don't wanna have a baby brother or sister. And I definitely, definitely don't wanna have another mother.

My dad called out from the bottom of the stairs, "I'm goin' to visit Grayce, Addie. I should be back in a few hours. Keep the front door locked."

"My dad's gettin' married," I said as I walked over to Rachel and sat down next to her on the love seat. I brought her the leftover pizza and some water, since that's all she drinks. I brought her some napkins and a plastic fork and knife in case she likes cutting the pizza. Some people do, not me.

"How come you're not happy, Addie?" She dabbed the corner of her mouth with the napkin.

"'Cause."

"'Cause why?"

"Just 'cause, that's all." Then I cried. I cried so hard, it was like a dam was burstin' inside me. Rachel took me in her arms and held me with all her might. She kept sayin', "Ssssh, ssssh, ssssh . . ." She kept sayin' it over and over. Then I cried more, 'cause it got me thinkin' that's what a mother does when a child's cryin'. She holds you in her arms and makes you feel better. She makes you feel like everything's gonna be okay.

I don't remember my mother ever holdin' me. Ever.

chapter thirteen

"I lied to you," Rachel said.

"What did you lie about, Rachel?"

"I lied about my parents, about them disowning me. They didn't. I ran away from home when I was seventeen. I never saw them again."

See now, this is what I don't understand about grown-ups. They're always sayin' to their kids, never, ever lie. Always. Like, for example, Joyce. She's always sayin' to Luke, "I don't want you lyin' to me. You can say anything, tell me anything, but don't ever lie to me." I don't think Luke tells Joyce too many lies, except, of course, little itty-bitty ones. Like he didn't tell her he got sick on candy at Halloween. But thinkin' about it, I don't think if you *don't* tell someone somethin', that's not a lie. That's just a secret. Secrets are way different than lies.

"How come you lied to me?"

"Well, I've been tellin' that story for so long, it just feels like the truth. But it's not the truth."

"That musta made your parents cry, don't you think?" She nodded.

"My mom ran away. When I was three years old, she ran away. My dad cried all the time. I would hear him cryin'. It made me real sad. I don't think runnin' away is a good thing. You shouldn't have done it."

"I wanted you to know the truth, Addie. I wanted to tell you 'cause I had a feeling your mom left you. And I want you to know somethin': I bet she feels really awful about that. I bet she thinks about you all the time and wishes she hadn't done it."

"Know what I think, Rachel? I think my mom left 'cause she really wanted to, and I stopped likin' her a long time ago, and I don't care if she thinks about me every single day for the rest of her life, 'cause you know why, she made me and my dad real, real sad. And I think when you think about someone all the time, you should try and find them and say hello, 'cause thinkin' about them doesn't make them feel any better. Besides, how do you know if someone's thinkin' about you if they don't tell you? I don't like that you lied to me, and I don't like that you ran away. I know what it's like to be run away from."

I wanted Rachel to leave. Her bein' around made me think too much, made me think about stuff I didn't wanna think about, like my mom. Ever since Rachel had been here, I was thinkin' about my mom more than I ever did. I shoulda never told her she could have some clothes, and I shoulda never let her stay here. I shoulda just fed her and let her shower and then said goodbye. I shoulda just done that.

"You can stay here tonight, but you gotta be gone in the morning," I said. "My dad usually gets up around nine on Sundays, so you should be gone by then."

I walked out of the barn and took my time goin' into the house.

My dad wasn't home yet. I went up to my room and sat on my bed, Indian style. Then I didn't wanna sit Indian style, 'cause it made me think of Rachel and I didn't wanna think about her, 'cause I was upset with her. I decided I should call Luke and tell him that Rachel's a liar.

You know what he said to me when I called? He said he didn't think Rachel's story was true when I told him in the first place. Said he had a six sense about it.

"A six sense, Luke?"

"No, Addie, a sixth sense. Like the movie."

"Wow. I liked that movie, Luke. That's my favorite movie ever. You tellin' me you're psychic?"

"I'm tellin' you I sorta felt like it wasn't true. I don't think I'm psychic, 'cause if I was, I woulda known my dad was gonna have a heart attack."

Good point.

"How come Luke, how come I didn't know she was lyin'?"

Then I heard Joyce callin' for him, tellin' him he hadda

get off the phone 'cause she wanted to call the hospital, see how Charlie was doin'. So he hung up the phone real quick without even sayin' goodbye. He does that sometimes—doesn't say goodbye, just hangs up the phone.

Sixth sense, huh? I'm not even a hundred percent sure my five others are workin' all that great.

I went upstairs and got into bed. I was just lyin' there, wishin' I could fall asleep. Musta been an hour later, I heard the car pull into the drive. Then I heard the door open and heard my dad walkin' up the stairs. I quickly closed my eyes, made believe I was sleepin'.

"You asleep, Addie?" he said. He was standin' by my door. I didn't answer. Then he walked away, and I musta fallen asleep, 'cause the next thing I knew, it was early mornin'.

chapter fourteen

"You have anything you wanna say to me, Addie?" my dad asked me.

"Uh-uh."

"Nothin'? Nothin' you wanna say?"

"Nope."

"Huh. I thought for sure you'd wanna say somethin' to me this mornin'. Maybe an apology or somethin'."

My dad looked up at me. Me and my dad, we sat at the kitchen table. He was readin' the *New York Times*. We get that on Sunday. He says he can read the *Pocono Record* every other day, but not on Sunday. I don't read the newspaper much. I figure anything I wanna know I can see on the news. I like watchin' TV. I don't like readin' the paper.

Luke, he reads the science section. Joyce always gives that section to him first thing. Sometimes he cuts out articles and thumbtacks them to the bulletin board in his bedroom. One time, I was at his house and he was showin' me this article on molecules and explainin' what it said. I went uh-huh, uh-huh, uh-huh. Didn't know what he was talkin' about.

Jessie sometimes, when she finds somethin' she likes, she reads it out loud to me. Like one time, she was readin' this story about some guy who won the lottery. He won a whole buncha money, like five or six million dollars. Anyway, he spent the money faster than you can say my name, and then what happened, he was so used to havin' so much money that when it was all gone and spent, he started robbin' banks. When he got caught, the police officer asked him why he did it, and he said he liked bein' rich. Jessie read me that story, and she was laughin' so hard she was cryin'. "What a fool," she said. "What a fool."

My dad was readin' the sports page. That's his favorite section. He'll sit and watch a football game on TV, and then the next day, he has to read about it. I don't get that. How come if you spend three hours watchin' somethin' on TV, you gotta read about it the next day? Seems you oughta read about somethin' you know nothin' about.

"I think you owe me an apology, Addie, and I was hopin' I would get it this mornin'."

See, this is what I don't understand. Somebody asks you if you have anything you wanna say, then you say uh-uh, nope, then they ask if you're sure, and then you say uh-huh, then they ask if you have anything you wanna say again, and then you say uh-uh again. How come when you say you have nothin' you wanna say, they keep askin'? Like the more they ask, maybe you'll wanna say somethin'? I don't get it. I just looked at my dad and thought, *How come grownups always, always, always think they're right?*

"I'm goin' to Luke's."

I didn't even wanna finish my eggs, and I'd made my very favorite type. Always make 'em on Sunday. They're my Sunday breakfast. For some reason—I'm not quite sure why—Sunday breakfasts are always sorta special. Like, for example, Jessie, she makes pancakes every single Sunday. Pancakes with bananas and all different kinda fruits, dependin' on the season. With real maple syrup. A coupla times when she hadda stay over on the weekend 'cause my dad was busy workin', she made pancakes. And I know for sure Joyce, she makes French toast every Sunday. I don't really like the way she makes 'em. For some reason they're real puffy, like she blew 'em up with somethin'. I like French toast when it's sorta crispy. Hers are definitely not crispy.

Scrambled eggs with American cheese, that's what I make on Sundays. What I do is this: I beat 'em, and I put in some milk and salt and pepper, and then I cut up pieces of American cheese and throw it in. Then I fry 'em. Tastes delicious. They're a little gooey, 'cause the cheese melts right into the eggs, but I like 'em fine that way. Anyway, I couldn't even finish my eggs. I kinda lost my appetite with my dad bein' so pushy about me talkin'.

I walked to Luke's. I was gonna ride my bike, but I knew I'd be doin' a lot of thinkin', and I figured if I rode my bike, I wouldn't be done thinkin' by the time I got there. When I was walkin', I thought about Rachel.

That morning I woke up really, really early, somethin' just sorta woke me straight up. Like one minute I was fast asleep, and then the next minute I wasn't. It was almost five-thirty in the mornin', 'cause I looked at my clock. The first thing that came to my mind was Rachel. I jumped right outta bed and went straight to the window, and there she was, walkin' away. I like when stuff like that happens— like you're thinkin' about someone for some reason, they just pop into your mind, and then the phone rings and it's them callin'. I just love when that happens. It feels magical. Anyway, there she was. I don't think she saw me watchin' her, 'cause I think if she did, she mighta stopped and waved. But I don't think she even looked up at my window. Her belly looked so big, and I started wonderin' if I did the right thing tellin' her to leave.

I'm not a hundred percent sure that her lyin' to me was really why I asked her to go. I think I was gettin' a little scared havin' her in the barn. I mean, even though my dad never, ever goes into the barn, sometimes people never, ever do somethin' and then decide to do it. Like Jessie, she always said she was never, ever gonna go on a plane. She said, "Ain't nothin' natural about eatin' a meal up in the sky." But one time, she hadda go to Florida in a big hurry, and she took a plane. So, you see, people say never, ever and then they do it. Maybe I was feelin' scared my dad's never ever time was up. But thinkin' about it, I think it's a good thing she's gone. Maybe she's gonna go back to the church. She seemed to like to pray, and that's the place to do it.

I was feelin' sorta sad and all. I watched her walkin' until I couldn't see her anymore. Then I got back into bed and tried goin' back to sleep, but I couldn't. And five-thirty in the mornin' is a little too early for me to be gettin' ready for the day. I remembered Luke told me when Joyce can't sleep, sometimes she'll drink a little bit of NyQuil—you know, the stuff you take when you have a cold and a cough. He says it makes her sleepy. She's always got a bottle of NyQuil in the medicine cabinet—the big economy size. Anyway, I went into the bathroom and looked to see if we had any. All we had was Tylenol and aspirin, and then a whole bunch of my dad's stuff, like shavin' cream and a razor, and some stuff of Grayce's, like lipstick and other kinds of makeup. So I just laid in bed, thinkin', thinkin', thinkin'.

I think the other reason I wanted Rachel to leave—and maybe it was the truest reason of all—was that she made me think about my mom a whole lot, and I'd gotten real used to not thinkin' about her. I was hopin' Rachel wouldn't think bad of me. Bein' that I was wide-awake, I went out to the barn. She'd cleaned up everything, which made me feel good. On top of bein' polite and gracious, she was also tidy. I sat down on the love seat, and I could feel my eyes gettin' all watery. I was gonna miss her; she was nice havin' around.

Just as I got to Luke's, I was done with my thoughts.

"Hey, Luke." He was sittin' on the porch. I sat down right next to him.

"Hey, Addie. We're goin' to visit my dad. Wanna come?"

"Uh-huh. Right now?"

"Uh-uh. Later."

"My dad's gettin' married."

Well, that just perked Joyce right up. She was inside the house and came right out.

"Myles is gettin' married?"

"Uh-huh."

"Good for him. She's a good woman, Grayce. I like her. She's got a nice flower shop, too, smells real good when you walk in. Somethin' about fresh flowers. Good for him."

"He never even told me he was gonna do that, just surprised me last night. I like her—I think she's nice and everything—but I can't say I'm happy he's gettin' married."

"Luke, honey, please do me a favor. Make me a cup of coffee. I only want one sugar this time. Last time you made me a cup, I almost went into shock."

"Can't you get it yourself, Ma? I got company."

"Addie's not company. Baby, when I ask you to do somethin', I got my reasons. Now go on, please."

Joyce always says please and thank you to Luke. I could tell Luke did not wanna be makin' Joyce a cup of coffee. Reason I know this, he slammed the screened door shut, and it don't have a latch, so it just kept bangin' and bangin'.

"One of these days, I'm gonna have to fix that. Charlie

was supposed to do it, but you know Charlie, middle name is lazy. You know how many things Charlie's put off doin'? I've lost count. I asked him to fix the toilet in the basement eight years ago. I said, 'Charlie, honey, that thing's leakin'; better fix it.' He just nods and says yeah, yeah, yeah. Toilet's still drippin'. I'm surprised this house hasn't sunk from all the water leakin' into the foundation."

She sat down right next to me. "Addie Goode, your daddy deserves a little happiness. Don't begrudge him that. You don't have to love her; he does. I always say to Luke, you don't have to agree with me, you don't have to like what I'm doin', all you have to show me is respect. R-E-S-P-E-C-T. God, I love that song. You know that song, Addie?" I know that song. Jessie plays it all the time. "Aretha. Now that's a woman doesn't take crap from any man." She started to sing the song, usin' her hands boppin' her head. Then she stopped. "I love that song, great song. Where was I? Oh, yeah, I think you owe that to your dad. He's given you everything he has. Now let somebody make him happy."

"I don't really wanna talk about this anymore."

"Addie, if you didn't wanna talk about it, you woulda never said anything about it in the first place. You just don't like me tellin' you that I think Myles deserves a little piece of happiness."

"That's a big fat lie. Besides, I make him happy. I love him. He thinks I need a mother, said so himself. Well, wanna know what I think? I think if he's marryin'

Grayce so that I can have a mother, he's makin' a big fat mistake."

Joyce looked at me—I mean, the kinda look when somebody has somethin' very important to say.

"He wants the best for you—"

"That's not—"

Joyce placed her hand smack over my mouth. "I wasn't finished with what I was gonna say, so don't you jump in and interrupt me. You wait till I'm done. He wants the best for you, but you ever think for one second that he needs a different kinda love than you have to give him? I'm not sayin' your love isn't enough. God knows you love him. I'm sayin' there's all different kinds of love a person needs: the love of a child, love of a friend, love of a parent, love of a lover. All kinds of love."

"I don't wanna talk about this anymore. If you wanna keep talkin', Joyce, go right ahead."

Luke came out with a steamin' hot cup of coffee for Joyce. "How many sugars, baby?"

He held up one finger and sat down next to me on the stoop. Joyce took a long sip. "Honey, you make a good cup of coffee. Some girl's gonna be real lucky to wake up to this smell one mornin'." She took another sip and sounded like she was purrin' like a cat. "I wanna stop at Luhrs on the way to the hospital, pick up a little gift for Charlie. Maybe you oughta think about buyin' him somethin' to perk him up a bit."

"Whaddya think he wants?" Luke asked.

"I don't know. Maybe you oughta get him a new wrench so he can fix that damn toilet when he's feelin' better."

Then Joyce looked at me, and we both cracked up laughin'. Luke just looked at us like we were crazy.

"What's so funny?" he said.

"Life's funny, Luke. Life's filled with funny."

Joyce went inside the house, and me and Luke we just stayed on the porch.

"Did Rachel leave?" Luke sorta whispered.

"Uh-huh. Really early, too. You think it's good I asked her to leave, or you think that was mean of me?"

"I think it's good. I gotta rake some leaves. You wanna help me?"

"How come you gotta do that now? More leaves are gonna fall soon, then you're gonna have to do it all over again. Why not do it just one time?"

"'Cause my mom asked me to. You wanna help, or you wanna watch?"

"I guess I'll help. If I help, will you do somethin' for me?"

"What?"

"I wanna go to the church, see if Rachel's there. I don't wanna talk to her or nothin'. I just wanna peek."

Joyce put on the stereo and played Aretha Franklin superloud. And on top of that, Joyce was singin' at the top of her lungs. When me and Luke stood up, we could see Joyce in the livin' room. She was dancin' all by herself—dancin' and singin'. Jessie's favorite sayin' in the whole world is

"Dance like nobody's watchin'." That's what she says. "Child, you gotta work like you don't need the money, love like you've never been hurt, and dance like nobody's watchin'."

Me and Luke, we walked to the church after he raked his yard. I held open the plastic garbage bags for him so he could put the leaves in. I know it doesn't sound like much help, but you know, without somebody holdin' those bags, the leaves can fly away. So really it's an important part of the leaf-rakin' process. We were just a little bit away from the church.

"Your mom never goes to church, does she?" I asked. "I mean, you don't go to church, so I'm guessin' she probably doesn't. Am I right?"

"Uh-huh. My mom and dad, mostly my mom, she studies Buddhism. Since she lived on that commune, that's what she believes."

"Do you believe in it, do you believe in Buddhism?"

"Sorta. It all makes sense. I mean, it's all based on cause and effect. And it's all about the fact that there aren't any coincidences in life. There's this book I read, *Buddhism and the Cosmos*. It's a big book—thick." He took his thumb and index finger and separated them about two inches wide. That's thick. I don't like thick books. I like 'em skinny with big print.

"How long it take you to read that book?"

Luke just shrugged. "I don't know. Two days?"

"Two days? It woulda taken me a whole year to read a

book that thick. It takes me two days to read a comic book, and that's mostly drawings. What's cause and effect mean, Luke?"

"Like, for example, you don't like studying, right?" I nodded. "So when you take a test, chances are you're gonna fail. So I guess the cause would be not studying, and the effect would be failin'. I think that's the simplest way of lookin' at it. It's way more complicated than that. Buddhists say you could have causes from a whole other lifetime and not get the effect until this lifetime."

"A whole other lifetime? I got enough issues with just the last three days. Now I gotta worry about other lifetimes?"

"You're silly, Addie. You know that?"

Just then, comin' out of the church, we saw Father Hall. He's gotta be almost eighty years old. We stopped walkin' and watched him. He's old and small and walks with a wooden cane that he made from a piece of tree limb. He carved it all by himself. This used to be his church. I suppose it still is, just nobody ever comes. I hadn't seen him in a long time. He mostly stays to himself. There's this little house that's sorta behind the church, in the distance. You can't see it, except maybe in the winter, when all the leaves are off the trees. Anyway, it's small, almost looks like a dollhouse, and that's where he lives.

Me and Luke watched him pickin' dead weeds by the front door. He just yanked 'em out and put 'em in a garbage can.

"Maybe we oughta not go any further, Luke. I don't think Rachel's inside."

Then Father Hall turned and said, "Who's there?"

I poked Luke in the ribs, and Luke poked me back, and I started to giggle.

"Who's there?"

"Me, Addie Goode. Me and Luke. We were just takin' a walk."

"Well, don't just stand there. Come and say hello."

He looked older close up, and smaller. He musta shrunk since the last time I saw him.

"You're bigger than I remember, the both of you. All grown up." Then he looked up at the sky. "It's gonna rain today."

The sky was all blue and clear.

"I don't think it's gonna rain today, Father Hall," Luke said.

"Oh, yes, it is. It's gonna come down in buckets today. It sure is. Well, good seein' you both." He started to walk away, and then he turned, looked up at the sky again, and then he looked right at us. "God doesn't question your existence," he said.

Me and Luke just stood there watchin' as Father Hall dragged the garbage can around to the back of the church.

"Well, Mr. Smarty-pants, Mr. Brains of the Bunch, what's that supposed to mean?"

"I don't know."

"A, B, C, D, E, F—"

"What word you lookin' for, Addie?"

"If I knew the word, Luke, I wouldn't be goin' through

the alphabet, now quiet, Luke, quiet . . . G, H, I, K, L, M, N, O, P, Q, R, S—got it, senile."

Me and Luke started walkin' back home. We were both a little quiet. When we reached the bridge, he turned to me and said, "You forgot the letter *J*." I just looked right at him, and thought to myself, *What? Huh?*

"The letter *J*. When you were goin' through the alphabet, you went, G, H, I, K."

I miss whole sentences sometimes. Someone could be talkin' to me, my mind wanders, and I can miss a whole paragraph.

"I just did that on purpose, Luke, see if you were payin' attention, that's all."

chapter fifteen

"Myles wants you to call, Addie. He's at home."

Joyce was all dressed up, lookin' really pretty for Charlie. She had on this peasant blouse—it had all sorts of embroidery on it. I really liked it. And I really liked her shoes. They were like little boots with laces all the way up.

"Where'd you get those shoes, Joyce?"

"These things? I've had 'em for years. I keep resolin' 'em. You like 'em?"

I nodded.

"Tell you what, when I get sick and tired of 'em, I'll give 'em to you."

I called my dad. He just wanted to know what my plans were for the day. I told him I was goin' to the hospital with Luke and Joyce, and then me and Luke were gonna play. Probably maybe go to the Kmart and play video games. He said okay. I said okay. He said he loved me, 'cause he always does, but this time it sounded more like he hadda say it. I told him I loved him, too. Then I hung up.

We stopped at Luhrs on the way to the hospital. It's sorta like an everything store, except it doesn't have clothes. It has toys and games and magazines and wallpaper and all sorts of home appliances, and it has a whole section devoted to hardware. Me and Luke, we played hide-and-seek while Joyce was shoppin'. A couple was lookin' to redo their kitchen, and what happened was, I hid in one of the cabinets, and they opened the one I was hidin' in, and the woman screamed, so I screamed right back. The man asked the salesman if the price included me. It was easy for Luke to find me. Joyce bought Charlie a stack of crossword puzzle magazines and a brand-new hunting cap. It was bright orange with earflaps. Pretty ugly, if you ask me. I think when Charlie goes huntin' and those animals see that hat, they're just gonna run away. Luke bought him a deck of cards so Charlie could play solitaire.

"That's all you're buyin' him, Luke? A deck of cards?" Joyce asked.

"He likes cards."

"Well, get it gift-wrapped. Go ask Jenny to wrap it for you. Tell her to put a nice big bow on it. That'll take the sting out when he opens it."

Me and Luke went over to where Jenny works. Sign says, CUSTOMER SERVICE. I don't know Jenny very well, only see her in town, but I know she lives in a trailer with her mom and her mom's boyfriend. And she's goin' to beauty school. That's all I know about her.

When we were standin' there, waitin' for her to wrap the cards, Cheryl came into the store with her new boyfriend, who had a Mohawk. His head was all shaved except in the middle, and he had a long earring in one ear. Well, at least I think it was her new boyfriend, 'cause I'd never seen him before. Last boyfriend she had, his name was Gary. He used to sit all day long in my dad's office waitin' for her to finish work. He'd just sit there, readin' magazines, and then when she wasn't on the phone, he would kiss her and tickle her and make her sit on his lap. My dad told me and Jessie that Gary was the runt of the litter. Anyway, they broke up. I don't know why.

"Hey, Addie."

"Hey, Cheryl."

"Hey, Luke."

Luke nodded. I don't think he likes Cheryl much. That's okay; he doesn't have to.

"What you doin' here?"

"Me and Luke and Joyce, we're goin' to the hospital to visit Charlie. He had a heart attack, but he's better now, so we're pickin up some presents. What you doin' here?"

"I'm paintin' my bedroom all red, like bright red—not that China red, but a bright red like blood—so we came here to pick up paint. I want you to meet Parker." Then she leaned in real close, right up to my ear, and said, "He's the coolest guy in the world. This is true love."

Then she turned and screamed, "Parker, honey, babe, come over here. I want you to meet someone." Everyone turned and looked at her 'cause she said it so loud.

He walked real slow. "Babe, this is Addie Goode, Myles's daughter," she said. He looked at her real strange, like he didn't know what she was talkin' about. "You know, my boss, Myles."

"Oh, yeah, yeah, right. Myles. Right. Yeah. How's it goin'? How you doin'?"

He had rings on all his fingers. Big silver rings, every single finger. And close up, the earring was a skeleton.

"I'm doin' fine, thank you, and yourself?"

"Man, I'm doin' great, just great, yeah, great. Yeah."

Then he kissed Cheryl. They were makin' out. Then he walked away real slow.

"Isn't he unbelievable? God, I hope when you grow up and you're ready to date, Addie, you find someone just like him."

If I grow up and date someone like him, I'm gonna throw up every single day.

"Addie, Luke, come on. Visitin' hours are startin'." Joyce was standin' by the door. Luke was still waitin' on his deck of cards. Seems Jenny kept rippin' the wrappin' paper and had to do it over and over again. She told Luke the cards were too tiny to wrap. I said goodbye to Cheryl but didn't bother sayin' goodbye to Parker. He was standin' and starin' at the wallpaper display, like in a trance or somethin'.

"Who was that you were talkin' to, Addie?" Joyce asked me while we were walkin' to her car.

"Cheryl, my dad's secretary."

"I didn't even recognize her. What did she do to herself? Somethin's different."

"It's probably the hair. It's a different color. Two weeks ago, it was orange."

"She keeps colorin' her hair like that, it's all gonna fall out one day."

"I don't think she'll mind. Don't you remember one time she shaved her whole head? Don't you remember that?"

"Vaguely. Why'd she shave it?"

"Said it was to protest the killin' of deer."

Luke just laughed and laughed. Me and Luke, we squeezed up front with Joyce. She was fidgetin' with the radio, and the Rolling Stones' song "Let It Bleed" was on. I know that song by heart, 'cause my dad, he always always plays the Rolling Stones. We all sang along, even Luke.

chapter sixteen

I hadda wait to see Charlie, 'cause only—what's that word . . . the nurse just said it—A, B, C, D, E, F, G, H, I— immediate, that's it, 'cause only immediate family could go in first. I'm not immediate family, even though I'm a friend. Maybe I guess I could even pass as a cousin or some-thin'. But I don't think cousins are immediate. I think they're in the same category as friends, so it wouldn't help if I was a cousin. Anyway, I hadda wait.

So I went into the waitin' room, and it was pretty empty. I shoulda bought a magazine at Luhrs—like I said earlier, all they had in the waitin' room was these health magazines. So I'm sittin', doin' a whole lot of nothin', and that man comes in. That older man from the other day who wore nice shoes. He sorta smiled at me, 'cause I think he remembered me. Least I think he did. So I smiled at him, then he nodded at me, and I nodded at him. Then he paced around the room. I was thinkin' of pacin' with him, just to sorta have somethin' to do, but he seemed like he wanted to pace alone. So I just watched him go back and forth, back and forth, back and forth. He seemed like a nice man. Even though he never, ever said anything, you can just tell when someone is nice. But sometimes you can think someone's nice, but they're not really. Like one time I was waitin' in line with Jessie at the bakery, and there was this woman there. She seemed nice. She was just standin' and waitin' in line, and I thought to myself, *She seems like a nice person.* And then what happened, the baker, he took someone else's order before hers. And she screamed at him real loud and told him that he shoulda waited on her 'cause she was first, And then she stormed outta there and said, "You can take your doughnuts and shove 'em."

I was wrong about her. Jessie says you can't judge a stew by the pot it's cookin' in.

The man stopped pacin' and went over to the vending machine for coffee. Now I can understand gettin' a soda from those machines, even candy, but coffee? Joyce always says there's nothin' like fresh coffee, and she once told me and Luke that the coffee in those machines is like mud. "You can stick a fork in it, and it'll stand straight up." Anyway, he got himself a cup and sat down. He didn't even sip it, just sat and stared at it. Maybe he was thinkin' he shouldn't drink it. Maybe when he looked into the cup and saw that it looked all muddy, maybe he thought, *I shoulda never bought this coffee.* Maybe that's what he was thinkin'.

Then a few other people came into the waitin' room. Now I wasn't sure if they were a family, but there was four of 'em. They didn't seem sad or anything, just loud. They talked real loud, like someone was deaf or somethin'. The man went up to the window and looked out. His back was to me, and I bet a hundred dollars that he was thinkin', *I wish those people would just shut up.* 'Cause that's what I was thinkin'. I wanted to say to them, *Excuse me, but I think the whole world can hear you.* A doctor came in, walked right up to the man, and tapped him on the shoulder. With those people talkin' real loud, it was hard for me to hear what the doctor was sayin', which I really, really wanted to do. All I could hear was him sayin' that the man's wife was doin' okay from the surgery and she was gonna be put in a room, but not a private room right away, 'cause the hospital was so crowded, so she was gonna have to share a room with someone. And I think he said temporarily, but those people were talkin' again. You ever wanna just punch someone in the arm and say, *Excuse me, I'm tryin' to overhear somethin' right now?* The man thanked the doctor, and the doctor said you're welcome, and then he said, "She's resting fine."

Luke came in and said I could visit with Charlie.

Charlie was wearin' the hunting cap and looked real silly. He had the flaps down over his ears, and I just giggled when I saw him.

"What's so funny, Addie Goode?"

"That hat, Charlie. That hat's ugly."

Joyce didn't like that I said that.

"Well, *you* don't have to wear it. Charlie does, and he likes it, don't you, babe?"

"Uh-huh. I love this hat, Joyce. Gonna wear it everywhere." Then Charlie flipped the flaps up. "I hear your dad's gettin' married."

Now you would think that Joyce and Charlie would be talkin' about somethin' else, like maybe his temperature.

"Addie's not happy he's gettin' married, so let's not talk about it."

"You're not happy, Addie? You should be happy. Weddings are nice. Me and Joyce have had a couple."

"We had one wedding, Charlie, and one elopement. I don't count that as a wedding. Come to think of it, a wedding is when you wear a long, white, flowing gown and carry a bouquet. I wasn't wearin' a white gown."

"What would you call what you were wearin'?"

"A caftan. And I carried daisies."

"But it was still a wedding." Then he took Joyce's hand and looked in her eyes for a long time. "You looked so beautiful, you know. When you stood next to me, I thought I died and went to heaven."

"And I thought, *Here comes hell.*"

Charlie laughed so hard I thought he was gonna have another heart attack. It was nice seein' him and Joyce laughin' together. There was a time, right after she threw him out, when he'd come over, and they wouldn't say one word to each other. A whole two hours could go by and not one word. Joyce would ignore him, and he would ignore her, and then they'd tell Luke to tell each other somethin', like "Luke, could you ask your father if he's done readin' the paper?" And Luke would turn his head and ask Charlie, and Charlie would say, "Tell your mother I'm not done yet." And Luke would turn his head and tell Joyce, and this would go on for a little while, even though they were sittin' across from each other. Luke always hated doin' that. So we made sure that when Charlie came over, we'd leave. But it's nice seein' 'em laughin'. They laugh good together.

Me and Luke, we stayed for a little while. It's sorta borin' bein' in a hospital—not much to do. When we were leavin', a nurse came in and said that Charlie was gonna have a roommate. And then she put new sheets on the empty bed.

When me and Luke were leavin' the hospital, my dad and Grayce were walkin' in. They were comin' to visit Charlie, and Grayce she had this big, big bouquet of flowers—all different kinds of flowers. It was so pretty. She makes pretty bouquets. I was just as nice to her as I always am, and she was just as nice to me. I told my dad that Luke and me were goin' back to his house and that I'd be home for supper.

"You have anything else you'd like to say to Grayce, Addie?"

"Nope, nothin' else." Then I turned to Grayce and said, "Is that okay with you that I have nothin' else to say?"

"That's fine with me, Addie. Just fine."

I turned to my dad, and I was so tempted to stick my tongue out at him, but I didn't.

Me and Luke went to Dottie and Sy's and had a big lunch. We didn't have any money, so Luke told Dottie that he'd bring her the money after school. She told him that she knew he was good for it and that she didn't expect he would be leavin' town in a hurry. I asked her if I could take a magazine and pay her after school. She told me that I still owed her for the last magazine I took. I don't remember that. But she took out a tiny pad, and written on it was that I still owed her $2.95.

"So how much will I owe you now?"

"Well, let's see. Two dollars and ninety-five cents and how much is that magazine you want?"

"Two dollars and fifty cents."

She took out a calculator, and before she could even punch in the numbers, Luke said, "Five dollars and forty-five cents."

"You're so smart, Luke," Dottie said and smiled at him. "So smart."

When we were walkin' home, it started to pour. It came down in buckets, just like Father Hall said it would.

"Maybe he watches The Weather Channel, Luke."

"You really think he has a TV, Addie?"

Then Luke and me, we looked at each other, and at the same exact moment, we both shook our heads no.

chapter seventeen

"Charlie seems in good spirits." My dad and me were doin' the dishes that night. I was dryin', and he was washin'. "Don't you think, Addie?"

"Uh-huh. Good spirits. Was he wearin' that hat when you saw him?" My dad nodded. "Do you think it's ugly?"

"I think huntin' is ugly."

"Me, too. Why do they have to kill deer?"

"For food, venison. Do you know that some people make venison jerkies—you know, like beef jerkies? Did you know that? Arnold makes venison jerkies. Never tasted one. Never plan to." Then he handed me a plate, and I dried it. "Did you ever meet Sam Batalin?"

"Nope. Who is he?"

"Used to be lawyer. Damn good one. Retired about two

years ago. Remember that big case coupla years back, a black fella was accused of murder, and it turned out he was railroaded? You remember that case?"

"Little bit."

"Well, Sam was the lawyer for the black fella, and he got him off. Anyway, I saw him today at the hospital. His wife's dyin' of cancer, doesn't have much time left. Doctors say she'll last another few weeks. He's so heartbroken. It's so sad."

"Where'd you see him?"

"His wife's sharin' a room with Charlie. They brought her in when we were there. That's when I saw him."

"What's he look like?"

"He's very dignified—tall, thin—"

"Does he wear nice clothes? Nice shoes?"

"I wasn't lookin' at his feet, Addie, but I imagine he does. He was always a very dapper man, a very sharp dresser."

"I think I sorta met him. I mean, we didn't talk or anything, but I think he was in the waitin' room when I was there. I think that mighta been him."

"They live over in Hawley—have this huge house right on Ellis Road, up from that fruit stand."

I musta stood there with my mouth open for a good five minutes. All I felt was sick—the kinda sick when your stomach gets into knots and you feel like you're gonna throw up but you know you're not gonna. But your belly is hurtin' so bad you feel like you gotta sit down or you're gonna fall down. That kinda sick. Almost like a scared sick.

"You okay, Addie?

"Uh-huh. It's just my belly."

"You don't look okay. You think it's somethin' you ate?"

"Uh-uh. I just feel funny, that's all. Just funny."

I took the forks and knives from my dad and dried them real slow.

"That house used to be a huntin' cabin, and they completely renovated it about fifteen years ago. Boy, what a job they did on that. Unbelievable! To take somethin' small and nondescript and make it special. What a house."

"I gotta go upstairs, Dad, and lie down. I think I may throw up."

"Well, you better lie down then. You want some Pepto-Bismol? I think there's some in the medicine cabinet." I just shook my head. "You're goin' to school tomorrow, Addie. You can't afford to miss another day."

"I know, I know."

I went into my bedroom and closed the door. I just sat on my bed, and all that kept goin' through my head was *Oh my God. Oh my God. Oh my God. Oh my God. Oh my God. Oh my God. Rachel's mom is gonna die.*

chapter eighteen

"Luke . . . Luke . . ." I was standin' right below his bedroom window. He keeps it open all the time, no matter what kinda weather we're havin', even snow. One time, we had a blizzard, it musta snowed at least twenty inches, and Luke kept his window open all night, and when he woke up, there was a pile of snow right in his bedroom. Joyce made him shovel it.

I was tryin' to be real quiet 'cause it was late. It was almost after ten o'clock, and I'm not even allowed to call him after nine-thirty on school nights. One time, I called there and Joyce said, "Do you know what time it is?" And I said, "Uh-huh." And she said, "Can't this wait for the mornin'?"

"Luke . . . LUKE . . ."

"Addie, is that you?" He stuck his head out the window.

"Luke, I gotta talk to you. It's real important—I mean, real big important."

"Okay."

I snuck outta my house in my pajamas. I put on a sweater 'cause it was startin' to get cold out, especially at night. I peeked into my dad's room, and it looked like he was fast asleep with all his clothes on. He does that a lot. Sometimes he'll even fall asleep on the couch and stay there all night. Jessie always says he could sleep through a tornado and wouldn't even know we had one until the next mornin'. But I bet if we had a tornado, he'd wake up. Maybe the tornado wouldn't wake him, but my screamin' would. Anyway, I tiptoed outta the house, and I took my bike and rode to Luke's.

"What's goin' on, Addie?" He was whisperin', so I whispered back.

"Luke, you're never ever gonna believe this. Charlie's sharin' his room at the hospital with Rachel's mom."

"Rachel's mom?"

"Uh-huh. She's got cancer, and she's gonna die. And she's gonna die real soon. And you remember that old man in the waitin' room? Well, his name's Sam Batalin, and he used to be a lawyer. You remember that case with the black guy who was accused of murder but he didn't murder anyone? You remember that? And you know what else? My dad knows him—he knows Sam Batalin and—"

"Wow! That is *so* weird. So cosmic."

"Luke, please don't get strange on me."

"You know what the chances of somethin' like this happenin' are? This is so weird. You get how weird this is?"

"I get it, Luke. But I need you to do me a big, big favor, okay?"

"I remember that black guy. He was really nice. I never thought he killed anyone. I liked—"

"Luke, I don't wanna talk about him. I need to talk about you doin' me a big favor, okay? Can we talk about the favor, please?"

"How big?"

"Humongous."

Luke scrunched up his face. "What is it?"

"I wanna go visit Charlie tomorrow after school 'cause I wanna see Rachel's mom. I mean, I'm not gonna talk to her or nothin', I just wanna peek. Okay? Will you do that with me? I mean, it really isn't that big a favor if you think about it 'cause you would probably visit Charlie anyway."

"I guess. I'll do it. It's not that big a favor."

"Well, sometimes, Luke, you say no, and I didn't want you to say no this time."

"Why you wanna see her?"

"I don't know. I just do."

"I only say no to my mom. I pretty much always say yes to you, Addie."

"Okay. Night, Luke."

I picked up my bike, and Luke whispered my name. "Addie."

"Uh-huh."

"I like your PJs. Pleasant dreams."

"You too, Luke."

I was tryin' to be real quiet when I got home—tiptoein' in and everything. But my dad, he was sittin' in the livin' room. His arms were folded across his chest, and the last time he folded his arms across his chest was 'cause he was very angry. But he wasn't angry with *me* that time. He was angry with Cheryl, though I'm not sure why but he was.

"Where were you?"

"I guess I went for a walk."

"You guess you went for a walk?"

"Uh-huh."

"At this hour? In your pajamas?"

"Maybe I was, what's that word I'm lookin' for—A, B, C, D, E, F . . ." But he didn't let me finish goin' through the alphabet. He just leaped right in.

"I was scared. I went into your room and you weren't there, and then I called your name and you didn't answer, and then I started worrying. It's not like you to just walk out of the house, Addie. When you're not feelin' good, you usually come into my bedroom." Then he stood up and walked right over to me. "Why don't I believe you?"

I was tryin' to finish goin' through the alphabet in my head—G, H, I, J, K, L, M—but he was just goin' on and on about not believin' me. I wanted to say, *Could you please be quiet for one second, 'cause I'm lookin' for a word?*

Then I finally got to *S,* and I said, "I was sleepwalkin'. That's what I was doin', sleepwalkin'."

"Really, is that so? Since when do you sleepwalk, Addie Goode?"

"I guess it's the first time. Maybe it'll become a habit now. Like maybe I'm gonna start sleepwalkin' every night. That's possible, isn't it?"

He just looked at me. It seemed like he was gonna start laughin', 'cause he had the start of this little smile, but then he got all mad again.

"I'm goin' to sleep, and I want you goin' into your room and we'll talk about this in the mornin'."

Uh-oh.

chapter nineteen

I was walkin' down the stairs to the kitchen, and I could hear my dad and Jessie talkin'. They were talkin' about my dad gettin' married, and he was sayin' that I was upset about that, and Jessie she sorta hollered, like a yahoo or somethin', and said, "You're gettin' married, Myles? Well, good for you." And then my dad said, "Thank you very much, Jessie," and then they went back to talkin' about me. I don't like bein' talked about behind my back when I can hear it.

Anyway, when I walked into the kitchen, they stopped talkin'. I wanted to say, *Excuse me, but I heard everything you said,* but I decided not to. I just said good mornin' to Jessie, and she said good mornin' pumpkin and then I said good mornin' to my dad, and he said good mornin'. And then I sat down at the table and waited for my breakfast. Jessie made grilled cheese with tomato.

"I want you comin' straight home from school today, Addie. Straight home."

"I can't. I promised Luke I'd visit Charlie with him, and I don't wanna break a promise to Luke. So I'll come straight home from school tomorrow, okay?"

"No, it's not okay."

"Charlie?" Jessie perked up right way.

My dad took a sip of coffee and then he said, "Charlie had a heart attack. He's in Trinity Hospital."

"Oh my Lord, a heart attack. Well, well, well. Wonder what made that happen?" Then she went over to the kitchen sink and started washin' the griddle.

"He's almost all better now," I said. Then I turned and looked right at my dad. "Anyway, I promised Luke I'd go with him and visit."

"Why do you think I want you to come straight home? Do you have a clue?"

"Uh-uh. Jessie, can I have a glass of milk, please?"

"'Cause you're bein' punished, that's why."

"Child, what you do?" Jessie placed the tallest glass of milk right in front of me.

"I guess it was 'cause I was sleepwalkin', and I guess I went right out of the house and went for a walk."

"That's right, Jessie, my daughter was sleepwalkin'. She was sleepwalkin' on her bike. You ever hear about someone sleepwalkin' on their bicycle?"

How'd he know I had my bike? I never saw him lookin' out the window when I came in. How'd he know?

Jessie laughed so hard she hadda lean up against the counter. Then she said, "You smell that, Myles?" Then she walked right up to me and started sniffin'. "I think it's comin' from you, sugar. Sure is, it's comin' from you." Then she sniffed one more time. "It's called horse manure."

My dad laughed, and Jessie she just kept laughin', but I didn't think it was funny. Uh-uh. I didn't know if I was turnin' bright red, but I sure felt like I was.

"I want you comin' straight home from school *today*, not tomorrow. You're just gonna have to break your promise to Luke, and I'm sure he'll understand." My dad stood up, folded his newspaper so he could put it in his briefcase, then he kissed me on the forehead. "I gotta get to work."

I wasn't hungry anymore.

"Sleepwalkin', child? Where'd you come up with that one? That's fresh."

"How do you know I wasn't?"

"Honey, just 'cause it was Halloween don't mean we're all livin' in pumpkin patches. I was married to a sleep-walker. He would sleepwalk right into the corner bar every night around eleven P.M. That's right. And in his sleepin' stupor, he would order a Scotch and water on the rocks. He tried sellin' me the same crap you are. Addie, it's not like you to make up stories."

"I'm not makin' up a story. I just got a big fat secret, that's all. You know how you always say to me keepin' a secret is a good thing if you want someone to trust you? You know how you always say that?"

"I sure do."

"Well, I'm keepin' a secret and my lips are sealed, and that's all I wanna say."

"Child, I wanna tell you somethin', and I want you listenin' to me and I want you lookin' at me when I talk to you. Right in my eyes." I looked at her. She has pretty eyes—real pretty. They sparkle. "I can count on one hand how many times you've fibbed—really told a whopper to your father. That's not like you makin' up stories. Now I'm not gonna ask you why you told that story, but I am gonna tell you that if you gotta lie to keep a secret, then the negative outweighs the good." Then she sat down and had this big grin on her face, and she was sorta whisperin'. "Now, sugar, how 'bout you tell me what this big secret is?"

"Uh-uh. My lips are sealed." Then I made believe I was zippin' my lips shut.

"You're not gonna tell me? Not even a tiny, little piece of it?"

I just shook my head, bein' that my mouth was zipped closed.

"How 'bout if I guess and you tell me if I'm right? That way, you're not really tellin' me the secret; I'm just guessin' it."

I just shook my head. I shook it so many times my head started hurtin'.

She looked at me. It felt like forever before she said another word.

"You come home by four o'clock. That'll give you an hour and a half to do whatever you gotta do. Now, go on, get to school."

I unzipped my mouth and said thank you.

chapter twenty

After school, me and Luke, we went to the hospital. I told him I was bein' punished for goin' out, told him that my dad knew I snuck out and that I better be home right at four o'clock, otherwise I'd get in big, big trouble.

"Just like Cinderella."

"I don't think so, Luke."

Charlie was all excited that Luke came to visit, 'cause he didn't expect him to, so it was like a big surprise. You shoulda seen his face. He musta been real, real lonely. There was this curtain closed between Charlie and the next bed. There was no noise comin' from the other side. It was all quiet.

While Charlie and Luke said hello, I sorta moved my way closer and closer to the other side of the curtain. There was Sam Batalin sittin' in a chair right by the bed, holdin' his wife's hand. She looked like she was sleepin'. Her head was all bald, like one of those Cabbage Patch Dolls. I have one. I named her Tutti-Frutti. Reason I named her that is 'cause Jessie said she looked like Little Richard without hair, and Jessie said I should call her Tutti-Frutti. I don't know who Little Richard is, but Jessie likes him, says he makes her howl. Anyway, there was a wig right on the night table next to her. It looked like it was sittin' on top of a big ball. Sam rubbed her face a few times and kissed her hand. I just stood there, feelin' very, very sad for him. Then he turned toward me.

"Hello," I said. He nodded. I said, "You know my dad, Myles, Myles Goode."

Then he said, "Yes, I do. I know him," and I said, "He likes you very much, said so himself." He seemed to smile when I said that.

Then he said, "You were the little girl in the waitin' room," and I said, "Uh-huh," and then I told him about Charlie and that Luke's my best friend and I didn't mean to intrude.

"What's your name?"

"Addie. Addie Goode. But you already know my last name, so you can just call me Addie."

"Hello, Addie, nice to meet you."

"Can I call you Sam, or do I have to call you Mr. Batalin?"

"Sam's fine."

"I'm sorry about your wife. My dad told me she's not feelin' very good."

"No, she's not."

"What's her name?"

"Françoise."

"That's a pretty name. Is that French?"

"Yes, it is."

I think he thought I musta been smart, bein' that I guessed that right. Then I told him that Luke speaks French, but not me. I'm takin' Spanish. All I know is a teeny bit. Not much at all. But Luke, Luke can speak French. Then I asked him if his wife was really French or just had a French name. He said she was really French, from France.

Then I heard Charlie askin' Luke who I was talkin' to, and Luke said Sam Batalin and Charlie asked who that was, and Luke said my dad knew Sam and Charlie said okay. Then Charlie said, "Addie always makes friends wherever she goes."

I walked over just a little bit closer to Françoise's bed, and all I kept thinkin' about was Rachel. I was gonna ask if they had any kids and see what he said, but I decided that probably wasn't a very nice thing to do. It might make him even sadder, and he was sad enough. All the time that he talked to me, he never ever let go of her hand. And lookin' at her, sleepin' and everything, I could tell she was real pretty. I didn't know what color eyes she had 'cause they were closed, but I imagined they were green, 'cause Rachel's eyes are green.

"Is she sleepin'?"

"Yes, she is. She's very tired. She's had a lot of tests done these past few days."

"I don't mean to bother you anymore. Very nice to meet you, Sam."

"It's very nice to meet you, Addie. Say hello to your dad for me."

I was just about to go back to visitin' Charlie and Luke when he said somethin' to me that almost made me cry. He said, "We had a daughter, but we lost her a long time ago. You remind me of her when she was younger." And then he turned his head away from me. I coulda sworn he started to cry.

Me and Luke, we took a shortcut home, bein' that I didn't have much time. I hardly said a word all the way. Luke kept askin', "What you thinkin', Addie? What you thinkin'? Why you so quiet?" Usually I'm the one askin' him what he's thinkin'.

"I gotta find Rachel."

"How you gonna find her, Addie?"

"I don't know, Luke, but I will."

I got home at ten to four, and Jessie was doin' her nails at the kitchen table. She was polishin' 'em a bright red.

"What color's that, Jessie?"

"Maybelline Jungle Red. Want me to do yours when I'm finished with mine?"

"Uh-huh."

I made myself a snack—Oreo cookies and milk. And I

dunked the cookies into the milk until they were soggy. I like 'em like that. I sat at the table next to Jessie.

"Glad to see you made it home in time. You take care of your secret?"

"Uh-huh."

I just looked at her. She sorta grinned at me. I just dunked my cookies.

"Did my dad call?"

She just shook her head. Then she blew on her nails so they would dry faster. "Okay, put your paws on the table and keep 'em spread."

How am I gonna find Rachel?

"Can I ask you somethin'?" I said.

"What is it, sugar?"

"How would you find someone if you didn't know how to find them?"

She looked at me sorta strange. "Like who?"

"No one."

"No one? You're lookin' for no one?"

"Never mind."

Then I thought to myself *America's Most Wanted.* That was it. Me and Luke, sometimes we watch that show when there's nothin' else on. Maybe they could help me find Rachel. They're always findin' people. Always. They have a number you can call. I think it's mostly if you seen the person that they show at the end of the program, but maybe they can find people for you. I'd have to ask Luke; he'd know.

"Stop movin' around. You're smudgin' your nails."

I musta been fidgetin' while I was thinkin'. I do that sometimes.

"Who's this no one you're lookin' for?"

"Never mind, Jessie. I got it all figured out. Can I ask you another question?" She nodded. "I wanna get a trainer bra. Could you go with me to Kmart? They have pink ones. I want one in pink."

She sorta leaned back in her chair and just stared at me. "You mean a training bra?"

"Uh-huh."

"Child, if you were any smaller, you'd be indented. You gotta be able to put somethin' in those bras, like me. A nice round D cup. It's what I like to call two handfuls. You got a teaspoonful."

"My titties are growin'."

"Only thing growin' these days is your imagination. Now blow on your nails. They're done." Then she stood up and grabbed her purse. "I'm goin' over to the Grand Union. We're havin' chicken for dinner. You stay put, you hear me?" I nodded. "Anything you need while I'm there?"

"Can you get me some soy milk, please?"

Jessie just stood with her hands on her hips, shakin' her head. "Soy milk, training bras, lookin' for no one—can't wait to see where this is headin'." Then she left.

"They only find criminals, Addie." That's what Luke said to me when I called him about my idea about *America's Most Wanted*. I didn't say anything after he said that, and then he asked me if I was okay. I said I was sad and he asked me why, and I said I didn't wanna talk about it anymore, and I hung up the phone.

I started to think about Françoise and Sam, and him holdin' her hand and not lettin' go, and him sayin' that they had a daughter but they lost her. And I believed in my whole heart that Rachel would wanna see her mom one more time before she died. I believed that so bad. And then it got me thinkin' about my mom leavin', 'cause my mom . . .

The phone rang and it was Luke, and he said he didn't like me bein' very sad, 'cause it made him very sad, and he wanted to know why I was sad. I started to cry, and then I told him. "'Cause my mom she left me forever, Luke, and I never, ever got to say goodbye to her."

chapter twenty-one

I wasn't hungry, but Jessie, she made her special chicken dinner with mashed potatoes. This time she added all this gravy, and I love gravy. My all-time favorite meal is on Thanksgivin'. Jessie makes the biggest, best turkey with stuffin' and gravy, and I eat so much of it my stomach blows up like a balloon. I always have to unzip my jeans 'cause my stomach's so big. I love her turkey. Oh, and you know what else? She puts these little paper booties on the turkey's legs. It looks so funny with those white booties. She only does that on Thanksgivin', 'cause Thanksgivin's special.

"How come you're not eatin', sugar?" she asked.

"Can I be excused, please?"

"You should eat somethin', Addie," Jessie said. I didn't feel like eatin', and mostly I didn't feel like sittin'. I don't know if you ever had this experience, but I felt like if I sat in that chair for five more minutes, I was gonna scream.

"Can I go for a bike ride?"

My dad looked at me. "A bike ride? Where you goin'?"

"Just out for a ride, nowhere special. Can I, please? I won't be long, I promise."

Then he asked me if I did my homework, and I said uh-huh, and he said okay, but just for one hour.

When I was walkin' toward the door, I could hear Jessie talkin' to my dad and she was sayin' that maybe I was goin' through somethin' hormonal, then she asked him if he noticed that I'd been very peculiar lately. My dad musta shook his head or nodded, one or the other, 'cause he didn't answer her. So I'm gonna guess that maybe he nodded just a little, just a tiny bit, not a big nod, just a mediocre one. And then Jessie said that when she's menstruatin', she's like Jekyll and Hyde. That's exactly what she said, she said, "I'm like a Jekyll and Hyde." I started gigglin'. I think the way Jessie says "menstruatin'" is funny. It sounds really, really long the way she says it. Like "mennnstruuuaaaatin'." I hadda cover my mouth, and all I could think was *All I got is a secret.*

Jessie hates when people have secrets. One time, I was listenin' to her on the phone with her sister, and she was yellin' real loud: "I can't believe you're not gonna tell me who you're seein'. I can't believe you're keepin' it a secret." Then she slammed the phone down and marched right outta the kitchen cursin' under her breath. She was cursin'

142

real quiet, but I heard it, and I asked her if she was mad at her sister for havin' a secret. And you know what she said? She said, "Child, I'm not mad that she has a secret. I'm just steamin' that she's keepin' it from me."

I got on my bike and rode straight to the church. "Excuse me, Father Hall?" He was cleanin' the altar when I walked in. Cleanin' and whistlin'. The candles were lit and it wasn't quite dark yet, and I thought to myself how pretty it all looked. Like magic.

"Excuse me." This time I said it real loud, like at the top of my lungs, and Father Hall turned around and looked at me kinda weird—the kinda look that sometimes someone gives you when they're not sure who you are or how they know you.

"Remember me, Addie Goode? Me and my friend Luke we were here—"

"Oh, yes, I remember. My memory's not so good these days."

"Mine either. I got short-term memory."

Then he picked up his cane and walked real slow-like toward me.

"I'm just gettin' old. Seems like just yesterday I was young."

Yesterday musta been a really long day, I thought.

"Can I ask you somethin'?" I said. He nodded. "I'm lookin' for someone, and I was wonderin' if you'd seen her. Have you seen her?"

"What's she look like?"

I described Rachel: her belly and her hair and the clothes she was wearin'. Then I mentioned maybe she was wearin' a big sweater, and he just shook his head.

"No one comes here anymore."

"My friend came here. She came here and she prayed."

He smiled, a little, teeny smile. Then he asked, "You ever see *The Wizard of Oz?*"

I said uh-huh, I did, and I told him that I loved that movie, except the part with those flyin' monkeys. I hated those monkeys. They were ugly, and they scared me. I remember the first time ever I saw that movie I had nightmares for two whole weeks that those monkeys were gonna come to my house. The Wicked Witch didn't scare me. Well, maybe when she took Toto. Wait a minute, she didn't take Toto. That Miss—A, B, C, D, E, F, G—Gooch, Miss Gooch, uh-uh, that's not it. But the same woman, she played both parts. It'll come to me. You know what he said? He said that he'd seen that movie at least twenty times. That's a lot of times to see a movie. Only movie I ever saw more than five times was *Babe*. I really like that movie. That little pig is so cute. Then Father Hall started whistlin' that Munchkin song—you know, the lollipop one—and then he stopped whistlin' and he said that Dorothy, that she took this real long journey, and when she was gonna go up in that balloon, the Good Witch—Glinda or Glenda, I keep forgettin'—anyway, she told Dorothy that all she had to do was click her heels together three times and repeat,

"There's no place like home. There's no place like home. There's no place like home . . ."

"I don't understand," I said.

"You will. Just remember, without faith, the Bible's just a book. I'm tired now. I gotta go home."

Then he walked over to the altar and blew out all the candles, one by one. Then he stopped, turned to me, and he tapped his heart three times, just like Dorothy tapped those ruby slippers. And he said, almost in a whisper, "It's all in here. All the answers are right here."

As he was just about to leave, I said, "Excuse me, Father Hall." He turned to me again. "How'd you know it was gonna rain?"

"My joints swell."

I rode my bike home. I tried not to get too scared about those monkeys, bein' that it was startin' to get dark and those kinda monkeys they come out at night. So I rode my bike faster and faster and faster, and I kept sayin' over and over again, "There's no place like home. There's no place like home. There's no place like home . . ."

Luke was sittin' on my porch, waitin' for me. Through the window, I could see my dad in the livin' room readin' a book. I saw him, but he didn't see me.

"Hey, Luke."

"Hey, Addie."

"Whatcha doin' here?"

"BLL 9987."

"Huh?"

"BLL 9987."

"You keep sayin' that. What is it?"

"Guess."

"You know I hate playin' this kinda game. It's always some kinda secret code or somethin', and I never ever get it right."

I sat down next to him on the stoop. "Come on, Addie, try. Please? Just once, try."

"Okay, fine." Then I just blurted out at least ten different things it coulda been, and every time he shook his head no.

"See that, Luke? I'm not good at these kinda games. So come on, what is it, huh, come on?"

"It's the creepy guy's license plate." I musta looked at him like, *What? Huh?* And then he said, "You can get an address off a license plate. You find out where he lives, and you'll find Rachel."

My mouth musta opened real wide, 'cause Luke said if it were any wider, a car could park in it.

"Oh my God. Luke, how'd you remember that, huh, how?"

He just smiled at me, then tapped his finger right on his brain.

"Guess what else, Addie?"

I didn't feel like playin' this game anymore, so I just shot Luke one of those "stop it" looks. And he said to me you don't have to guess but I'll tell you, he said that Miss Sinclair, that she works over at the motor vehicle department, and the reason he knows that is 'cause Joyce, she had an accident last year. She was comin' outta a parkin' space at the Grand Union, and she backed right into the car behind her. Smashed the person's lights and everything. She hadda go to the motor vehicle place, and Miss Sinclair, she was the one she hadda talk to.

I said to Luke, "Miss Sinclair? She's mean. We don't like her."

And you know what he said? He said, "Now we do."

Then I leaned over and kissed him on the cheek. Sometimes Luke'll wipe it off when I do that, but this time, this time he didn't.

chapter twenty-two

The next mornin', I walked over to Luke's to pick him up so we could go to school together. Joyce answered the door and she was wearin' a short, red wig. She asked me what I thought. I told her straight out I didn't like it. Sometimes Joyce'll wear a wig 'cause she's thinkin' about cuttin' her hair, and instead of cuttin' it, she'll just put a wig on. Her sister, Patsy, she works in a beauty salon down in Philadelphia, and she sends Joyce all these wigs. One time, a few years ago, I was sleepin' over at Luke's, and Joyce and Charlie were listenin' to this record. They were listenin' to "Do You Believe In Magic?" I can't remember the name of the band—wait a second, A, B, C, D, E, F, G, H, I, J, K, L—I got it, the Lovin' Spoonful. Anyway, they were singin' along, and then Joyce she went and got four wigs from her bedroom and she gave each one of us one to wear, and we made believe we were the group. I had on a long, blond one and Luke wore a dark one with a flip, and Charlie wore a short, curly, brown one. And Joyce wore an Afro.

"I kinda like this one, Addie," Joyce said. "Bein' a red-head makes me feel sexy. You sure you don't like it?"

"I'm sure. How come it makes you feel sexy?"

Joyce touched the wig and kinda shrugged. Then she yelled up to Luke's bedroom and told him I was waitin' for him, and Luke he came hurryin' down the stairs. We were just about to leave but then Joyce stood right in front of the door and she said, "Not so fast, buddy. First you gotta plant one right here." And she pointed right to her cheek. Luke kissed her goodbye. Then she asked him what he thought of the wig, and he just shook his head.

"Now go on. You have a good day, the two of you. And remember, Luke, I'm workin' at Pete's doin' a double, so I won't be home till ten."

At lunchtime, me and Luke we went to Dottie and Sy's and I had a hamburger and Luke had a tuna melt, and then we discussed how we were gonna get the address from Miss Sinclair. And then you'll never believe what happened, but it did, cross my heart. Miss Sinclair walked into Dottie and Sy's and sat down right at the counter. I was sorta starin' at her for a little bit, and then she turned to me and said, "What you starin' at, Addie Goode?" I said nothin', and she said, "You callin' me a nothin'?" and I said uh-uh, that's not what I meant. Then Luke punched me in the thigh, and I turned to him and he motioned for me to zip up my mouth, so I did.

Luke whispered in my ear, "I got it," and he got up off his stool and walked right over to Miss Sinclair. He very politely said that he was tryin' to find a friend of his, a friend from camp but he didn't have the address but he did have his friend's father's license plate.

Miss Sinclair looked at him real peculiar. "You have his license plate? That's a bit odd, don't you think, Lucas?"

I thought Luke was gonna punch her, her callin' him Lucas, but instead he just said, "Well, my friend and me, we used to play this game called States. You hadda guess the state from the license plate, and he gave me his dad's license plate number, and that's how I have it."

"That's an odd game. I never heard of it," Miss Sinclair said. Then she ordered pancakes with bacon and extra syrup.

"Well, we sorta made it up. Anyway, do you think you could help me find his address, please?"

She stared at him. Her eyes got real small and beady. "You come by after school."

Luke said thank you and went back to his stool. And then Miss Sinclair she turned to me and I musta been starin' at her again 'cause she said, "You know what happens to people who stare? Their eyes get stuck open, and they can never blink again."

Gulch. Miss Gulch. That's who took Toto.

chapter twenty-three

Me and Luke, we went to the motor vehicle place. It's on Broad Street, right next to the police station. And not too far away and across the street is my dad's office. I started thinkin' what if, what if, what if we ran into my dad. Luke said if I stopped thinkin' about it, then it wouldn't happen. But if I thought about it too much, I could make it happen. So I just shook that thought right outta my head.

There were a buncha people at the motor vehicle place—high school students takin' some kinda eye test. Luke told me they were doin' that so they could get their driver's permit. And Luther was there, still wearin' a bandage on his nose and everybody, everybody seemed grouchy. Like I said hello to Luther, and it seemed like he growled at me.

Luke told me that when Joyce hadda go there, she waited

for almost two hours in line. Joyce hates standin' in line. Lots of times she'll cut ahead. Uh-huh. Like one time, we were at the movie theater—we went to see *Titanic*—and there was this line around the block. You know what Joyce did? She snuck up to the front of the line that was movin', goin' into the theater, and she told this man who was just about to walk in that she'd been waitin' for over an hour and hadda go pee and had asked me and Luke to hold the place, but that we had gone off to play. That's what she said, that me and Luke had gone off to play. And then she smiled at the man—and Joyce has this real nice smile—and he let her cut ahead. Then she waved us over. The man looked at us funny, and Luke asked Joyce why, and she whispered to him what she had said. Luke asked her why she blamed us, and she said, "Honey, sometimes you gotta blame someone," but that she would buy us the biggest tub of popcorn and Twizzlers, 'cause they're my very favorite.

Anyway, Luke went up to the person at the desk and said we were here to see Miss Sinclair, and the person said okay but we had to wait, so we did.

When Miss Sinclair came out, Luke gave her the license plate number, and she wrote it down on a pad and then she asked what the name of his friend was, and Luke looked at me. So I looked at Luke, then he widened his eyes, so I widened my eyes. "What's the name of your friend, Lucas?"

"I need to talk to Addie for a minute," he said. "We'll be right back."

Then Luke he almost dragged me out of the chair and pulled me across to the other side of the room.

"Luke, whaddya doin'?" I said real loud.

Luke put his hand over my mouth and started whisperin'. "Ssssh, Addie. What's the name of the guy, Addie? The creepy guy?"

"I don't remember. How come *you* don't remember? *You* got the photographic memory."

"You never told me his name, Addie. If you told me, I would remember. Start goin' through the alphabet."

"I did, too, tell you, Luke. No way am I gonna remember now under all this pressure. No way. I can go through the alphabet a hundred times straight, and I won't remember."

"Try."

"I'm goin' to the bathroom." I started walkin', then turned to Luke. "You comin'?"

I went into the ladies' room, and Luke followed me right in. It's just big enough for one person—one toilet and a sink and that's it. I locked the door, and I went through the alphabet over and over and over again.

"Nothin'. I don't remember his name. I'm sorry, Luke. Now what?"

"I know. I'm gonna tell Miss Sinclair you got sick and you're throwin' up, and I gotta take you home."

"She'll never believe that, Luke."

Me and Luke, we went back to Miss Sinclair. He told her that I wasn't feelin' very good and that we'd come back for the address when I was feelin' better. She looked at me. I tried to look sick, but I wasn't really lookin' very sick. Then she looked at Luke with her small, beady eyes. And then she turned to look at me again and said, "You don't look very sick, Addie."

"I just threw up. Want me to throw up now?"

"You're a little smart-ass, aren't you, Addie?"

You know what I wanted to do? I wanted to say to her right at that very moment, right in her face, *Miss Sinclair, I know your secret. Na na na na na.* But if I did that, you know what woulda happened? She woulda called my dad and probably definitely screamed at him. And then he woulda asked what I was doin' there in the first place, and she woulda said lookin' for an address, and I don't even wanna think about the rest of it.

So me and Luke, we went to the hospital to visit Charlie and when we got there, Françoise wasn't in the next bed, and my heart stopped, 'cause I thought maybe she died. So I asked Charlie where she was, and Charlie said she was havin' some tests done. Then my heart felt better. Then he asked me how I knew her and I told him that my dad knew Sam and that Sam was her husband, and then Luke said to him, "Remember, I told you?" and he nodded.

Charlie was playin' solitaire when we got there. He was puttin' jacks on top of kings and sixes on top of eights. I asked him how come he was cheatin', and he said, "You're allowed to cheat when you play alone." Me and Luke we only stayed for a little bit, and then we walked back to Luke's house.

"Now what, Luke, huh, now what?"

Luke made me and him a snack. We had chocolate chip cookies and vanilla ice cream, and what we did was put the ice cream between two cookies and made these little sandwiches.

We each had a glass of milk. Luke didn't answer me right away, which means he was thinkin' about the answer.

"How much money you got, Addie?"

"Right now, this very minute?"

"No, how much you got saved?"

I told him maybe eight dollars, but mostly in dimes and nickels and then he said he had about thirty dollars, mostly in dollars and fives and I asked where he got the fives from, and he said he gets five dollars for his birthday from his grandma and grandpa. I just get pajamas. Every year, my grandma and grandpa send me new pajamas. I'm gonna ask them to send me money next birthday. Then I asked him why he was askin', and he said 'cause maybe what we could do was go on the Internet and go to spy.com and then he said that they give you all sorts of information, like findin' a missin' person or locatin' someone who moved. Then he said they can even let you know if someone has a criminal record.

"Oh my God, Luke. Oh my God. I wanna find out if that creep's a criminal. I bet he is. I just bet. I got a sixth sense about it."

"Addie, let's just give 'em the license plate, get a name and an address first."

"Then can we—?"

"Uh-huh."

Since me and Luke don't have a credit card, he said maybe what we could do was send them a money order, then in a few days we could go online and get the information.

"That's genius, Luke."

"I know."

Then we made some more cookie sandwiches.

chapter twenty-four

I was sittin' on my bed, doin' my homework, when Jessie just stopped and stood in my doorway. She was just standin' there, hands on her hips, shakin' her head, doin' this clickin' thing with her tongue. She does that to get your attention if you're not payin' attention to her. She clicks her tongue. And sometimes, if you're ignorin' her, she does it real loud. Then she walked into my room and stood over my bed, starin' down at me.

"My birthday's comin' up. You know what that means, Addie?"

"It means we're gonna have a birthday cake with a lot of candles so you can blow 'em out and make a wish."

"It means it's time for me to renew my driver's license."

Uh-oh.

She seemed a whole lot bigger lookin' down at me. Like

she was this giant, and I was like this teeny person. Like in *Gulliver's Travels.* I decided it would be a good thing not to look at her. So I just kept my head down, doin' my math.

"Ain't you just a little curious where this is headin', child?"

"Uh-uh."

"Uh-uh? Uh-uh? I saw you and Luke comin' out of Miss Ramona Sinclair's office today. And I went in there and I said to her, 'Ramona, what was my little sugar doin' in your office?' And she told me some cock-and-bull story, that you and Luke we're lookin' for a camp friend."

"So?"

"So?"

"It's Luke's friend. A friend from camp. He lost the address and he had a license plate number—"

"Stop it right there, right now and you look at me right this minute, you hear me? I wanna look into those eyes of yours and see if they're dilatin'. Come on."

I looked up at her. I could feel this lump gettin' stuck in my throat, like I swallowed a gumball whole and it was just sittin' there not movin'.

She stared right into my eyes. "I can see it. It's right there, right in the center of your pupils. You becomin' a better liar than my ex, and, honey, he's already won first prize. Who is this person you lookin' for? And don't you lie to me, 'cause my antenna is way up."

"If I tell you the truth, you swear, you promise, you cross your heart and hope to die?"

"I swear and I promise, but I ain't crossin' no heart of mine and hopin' to die."

Then I got up off my bed and closed my door. I told Jessie everything, from the first time I saw Rachel to bringin' her home for breakfast to hidin' her in the barn to her bein' pregnant. I told her that when me and Luke saw her in the church—the old church by the river road—that she was bein' beaten by this creepy guy. I told her about Sam Batalin and Françoise and that Françoise was gonna die and that I wanted to find Rachel so she could say good-bye to her. And then I said that was the whole truth, that was our secret, me and Luke's. And then I asked her if she was gonna tell my dad, and she just looked at me. The kinda look that makes you think that maybe, maybe that person is thinkin' about tellin' on you. My chin started to quiver, and I just looked at her with these puppy-dog eyes that were ready to burst out cryin'.

"You told me walkin' away from evil is just as evil, Jessie. That's what you told me. Don't you remember, huh?"

Jessie didn't say anything to me. She walked out and closed the door behind her. I could hear her walkin' down the stairs, and then I didn't hear anything anymore, except my heart poundin'. It was poundin' so fast and so loud, I thought it was gonna pop right outta me.

chapter twenty-five

Jessie didn't say a word to me at breakfast the next day, not one word. My dad had already gone to work, and it was just me and her. She was doin' the dishes and foldin' clothes from the basket and not sayin' a word. I hate when she does that. I hate it.

Just as I was about to leave for school, just as I was about to walk out, she said, "How were you plannin' to go find your friend, that girl, what's her name?"

"I guess we woulda taken a bus or somethin'."

"We?"

"Me and Luke. You should start usin' the alphabet. A, B, C, D, E, F—"

"*S,* as in stop it right now, the two of you, you two little Sherlocks."

"*R,* as in Rachel." Then I left.

I picked up Luke at his house, and when we were walkin', I told him that we got caught by Jessie, that she was at the motor vehicle place and talked to Miss Sinclair, and that I told her everything and I hoped he wasn't mad at me for not keepin' our secret.

"I'm not mad at you."

"Honest?"

"Honest."

By the fourth period, I hadn't heard one single word any of my teachers had said. Not one. Finally, I raised my hand and asked Miss Hansen if I could be excused. She asked me why, and I said 'cause, and she said 'cause why, and I said 'cause I hadda pee and I couldn't hold it in anymore and everyone laughed. Then she said I could be excused.

I ran to the bathroom and looked under all the stalls to see if anyone was in there. Then I went into a stall and I closed the door and I put the toilet seat down. I sat on it and then I said quiet but not too quiet, "I know I haven't been talkin' to you in a real long time, and I'm gonna tell you why, so I hope you're listenin', 'cause maybe you stop listenin' to people who stop talkin' to you. But you see, I prayed for my mom to come home. I prayed every day for a whole two years, and my mom, she never, ever came home. So I stopped talkin' to you, and now I got another favor, and I sure hope you're hearin' me, 'cause it's big and it's important."

Then I started to cry; I just couldn't help myself. I took some toilet paper and blew my nose, and then I said, "Please,

please, please don't let Françoise die before I find Rachel. I don't know why this is so important to me, but it is, and I just really, really need to find Rachel and please, please, please can you please help me? I don't know how you can, but I sure hope you will. Thank you very much for listenin'."

I sat in the bathroom for a little while longer. I blew my nose one more time and wiped my eyes.

When I got back to class, Miss Hansen asked me if I was okay. I said uh-huh and sat down in my seat.

chapter twenty-six

Me and Luke, we walked to the post office right after school. I told him all about me prayin' to God.

He said, "You did?" And I said uh-huh, and I prayed out loud, too. But not too loud, just enough. And he asked me, "Where'd you pray, Addie?" and I told him the bathroom, and then he started to giggle, and I didn't think that was very funny, so he stopped gigglin' real fast. I told him that I wasn't sure if God was listenin' to me. Then he said, "You know what I think, Addie? I think that when you say somethin' out loud, somebody's bound to hear you."

The post office is the tiniest place you ever seen. It's like a small dollhouse, except people fit in it. But barely. Me and Luke, we were standin' so close together, we coulda been Siamese twins. Clive works at the post office. Durin' the day, he's the mailman. Then after he delivers all the mail, he works at the post office. I like Clive. It was his sixty-fifth birthday last year, and everybody left a birthday card for him in their mailbox. He's real tall and skinny, like a stick figure. And he's almost deaf, so he talks real loud, and then you have to talk real loud. When Clive and Sy get together, all they do is scream at each other.

"Hey, Luke. Hey, Addie."

"Hey, Clive."

"Hey, Clive."

"Somethin' you kids need?"

Luke took all the money out of his pants pocket. "We need a money order, Clive. A thirty-five-dollar money order and one stamp, please."

"How much?"

Then Luke said real, real loud and real slow, "Thirty-five dollars, Clive."

"Whaddya kids buyin'?"

"Can't tell you. It's a secret," I said real loud. Luke started gigglin'. He said it was funny that I was sayin' it's a secret that loud.

"Good thing I don't write out the money order, then it wouldn't be much of a secret, would it, Addie?"

"Guess not."

"Huh?"

I just shook my head. I didn't feel like sayin' "guess not" again. Clive was writin' up the money order, then he said, "Luke, you see the lunar eclipse the other night?"

"Uh-huh."

"What's that you say, Luke?"

"I said yes, I saw it."

"Me and Katie, we were sittin' outside on the porch, drinkin' some beers, starin' up at that big sky. Here's your money order." He handed it to Luke.

"We need a stamp, Clive." Clive handed Luke one stamp.

Luke took out his pen and wrote "spy.com" on the money order. Then he took an envelope out of his book bag—he had already written the address on it—and he stuck the money order in it and gave me the envelope to lick. I told him uh-uh, I didn't wanna lick the envelope 'cause I hate the way it tastes.

"You gotta do somethin', Addie."

Ick.

Then he put the stamp on it and handed it to Clive.

I looked at Clive and said real loud, "Better not look at that envelope. It's a secret, remember?"

"I don't know what you're up to, but sure makes me wanna be young again."

"Bye, Clive."

"Bye, Addie."

"Bye, Clive."

"Bye, Luke."

When I got home, Jessie, she was sittin' at the kitchen table. There were Oreos and milk waitin' for me.

"How much homework you got, child?"

"Some."

"Get to it."

"Now? I don't like doin' homework the minute I get home."

She gave me one of those looks, the kinda look that sorta says, *Addie Goode, I'm not in the mood for this.* So I gave her one of my looks back that said, *I don't care what you think.* She tapped the kitchen table with her nails. Then I dunked a cookie in the milk and waited till it got all soggy.

I did my homework. When I finished, I gave it to her to look at and she read it and said I did good.

"Where's Luke?"

"Home."

"You go call him. Ask him to come here."

"You gonna yell at at him for havin' a secret with me?"

She just pointed to the phone.

I called Luke and I told him that Jessie wanted to see him and you know what he said to me? He said, "Is she gonna yell at me for our secret?" and I said I don't know but I think you better get here.

Luke came by about ten minutes later. Me and Luke we sat at the kitchen table. Jessie sat across from us, just sorta lookin' at us. She shook her head a few times and then she let out a sigh—a real big sigh. My belly was startin' to hurt real bad.

Jessie stood up and said, "Come on, both of you."

I knew it. I just knew it. I shoulda made her cross her heart and hope to die, I just knew it. She was gonna take me and Luke to my dad's office and make us tell him the whole story. I just knew it. Then he was gonna punish me for the rest of my life. No TV, no telephone, no snacks, no nothin'. Just school and homework. My belly was hurtin' more than ever. Next time, I don't care what she says. If she don't cross her heart and hope to die, I'm keepin' my mouth shut.

"Where we goin'?" Luke's voice was tremblin' when he asked.

Jessie grabbed her purse and her keys and held the door open for us. Me and Luke looked at each other. He looked like he was gonna pee in his pants, and I was gettin' ready to throw up. Finally, I just blurted out, "Can't we just call my dad? Please, please, pretty please? Can't we just do that? Can't we just call him? I don't wanna go see him. Pretty please?"

Me and Luke followed Jessie to the car like two little puppies. She opened the back door, and we got in. Me and Luke just looked at each other. I was holdin' my breath. I was so afraid to breathe, I can't even begin to tell you. Jessie drove through town, and when we passed Broad Street and didn't stop, I felt like I was lettin' out a year of breathin'. Then we came to a sign that said, HAWLEY 10 MILES, and it had an arrow pointin' one way. On the same sign, it said, MARSHALLS CREEK 30 MILES, with an arrow pointin' the other way. We turned where the arrow was pointin' to Marshalls Creek. I could see Jessie lookin' at me in the rearview mirror. She just looked at me for one quick second. Luke took my hand and squeezed it real tight, and I squeezed his hand back.

chapter twenty-seven

Jessie was drivin' real slow as soon as we got to Marshalls Creek. Marshalls Creek is ugly, and on top of that, it looks dirty. Like someone came along and dropped a ton of dirt on everything. The houses are small and real close together, and I bet if you're standin' in your house and lookin' out the window, you can see right into the next person's house and watch everything they're doin'.

"2342 Liberty Road. 2342 Liberty Road. 2342 Liberty Road. 2342 Liberty Road." Jessie kept sayin' it over and over again. We were drivin' so slow that the person behind us was honkin' the horn. I turned around and looked out the back window, and I could see a girl drivin' and next to her was a guy, and she just kept blowin' her horn, and it was just goin' and goin' and goin'. Finally, Jessie got so mad, she pulled over, rolled down the window, and screamed, "Hey, girlfriend, lay off the horn. None of us is deaf." Me and Luke started gigglin', and then Jessie, she started gigglin'.

We pulled into a gas station, and Jessie asked the man to fill 'er up. Then she asked where Liberty Road was, and she turned to Luke and said, "Could you please pay attention to the directions?"

The man gave us directions, then he said to Jessie, "Thanks for stoppin' in, honey," and winked at her.

"How come he winked at you, Jessie, huh, how come?" I said.

"Sugar, that poor fool's been workin' that gas station so long, he's mistakin' a fill 'er up for a date."

When we pulled onto Liberty Road, all the houses looked like they needed repairs. Then I saw it. I saw the creepy guy's truck sittin' in a driveway. My mouth musta opened real wide. I couldn't even speak. I punched Luke in the thigh, and when he turned to me, all I could do was point at the truck. His eyes widened, and he turned to me. I could see Jessie lookin' at us in the rearview mirror.

"You want me to go in with you, Addie?" Luke asked. I shook my head.

"You want me to go, sugar? You want me goin' with you?" I shook my head at Jessie.

I got outta the car and walked across the street. The closer I got to the house, the more scared I got. My heart was tremblin' and my knees were tremblin' and I turned around and looked at Jessie. She was just sittin' there, watchin' me through the windshield. Then she smiled at me, and I felt better. I felt safer.

I rang the doorbell. Then I took a step back and waited for someone to open the door. I could see through the window, through the curtains, that the TV was on, and so I rang the bell again. I could hear some man screamin', "Answer the goddamn door." And then the door opened, and the only thing separatin' me and the creepy guy was a screen door. He looked at me, he looked me up and down, and said, "Yeah, whaddya want?" I asked if Rachel was home and then he looked at me again and said, "I know you. Where do I know you from?" I said I don't really know you and he said, "Don't lie to me. I know I seen you somewhere." I said you don't know me but you seen me, and I just wanted to see Rachel if that's okay. Then he turned and screamed, "Rachel, Rachel, Rachel," at the top of his lungs and then the same man who'd screamed before screamed back at him, askin' who was at the door, and he said someone for Rachel. Then he screamed Rachel's name again, turned back to look at me, and said, "I don't know where she is" and I said I'd be sittin' on the stoop waitin'. Then he slammed the door closed.

I sat down on the stoop and looked over at the car. I waved at Jessie and Luke, and they waved back at me. And I just waited. It felt like hours, but it musta been just a few minutes. Then the door opened, but I didn't turn around. Then I heard the screen door open, and I turned, and Rachel was standin' there. When she saw it was me waitin' for her, she smiled this big smile and she sat down next to me.

"How'd you find me, Addie?"

"Jessie, she found you." I pointed to the car where Jessie and Luke were.

"Whatcha doin' here?"

I told her about my dad knowin' her dad and me meetin' him at the hospital and her mom bein' so sick—so very, very sick—and everything. She started to cry, but it was the kinda cryin' when you try and hold it in. Then I said I thought maybe she'd wanna see her mom one more time. I said nothin' else, and we just sat there. She wiped her eyes with her hand, and then she got up off the stoop and asked me if I could wait a minute, if that would be okay. I told her that I was gonna go to the car, that I didn't like sittin' on the stoop, and that I didn't want her to take that personal.

Rachel went back inside, and I walked back to the car. When she came back out again, I heard the creepy guy say, "You better be askin' for some money, Rachel. You better not come back empty-handed, you hear me? You hear me?"

As Rachel walked to the car, the creep just stood on the stoop screamin' at her. She didn't even look at him, not once, she just kept walkin', and he just kept screamin', "You better not come back empty-handed, you hear me?" I could hear Jessie say under her breath, "Poor child. Poor, poor child."

Me and Luke we sat in the back, and Rachel sat up front

with Jessie. Jessie told Rachel that years ago, when she was in her twenties, she was a midwife. I never knew that. She said she delivered eight babies—five girls and three boys. She said one of the boys came out premature and that he hadda be in an incubator for a whole month, but he was okay after that. Then Jessie put her hand on Rachel's belly, and she said that Rachel was gonna have a baby girl, that she could tell.

"A girl?" Rachel said.

"Yes, ma'am, you gonna have a girl. I can feel it." Jessie looked at Rachel out of the corner of her eye. "You oughta put somethin' in your stomach. That baby needs nourishment."

We stopped at a diner on the way home. Me and Luke we only had chocolate malteds, 'cause Jessie said we shouldn't ruin our appetites for dinner. Luke said Joyce was makin' macaroni and cheese and that he hated macaroni and cheese, so he didn't care if his appetite was ruined. "But your momma will, Luke, so keep some room in that belly of yours." That's what Jessie said. Rachel, she had a tuna melt and French fries and onion rings and a salad. She didn't leave one thing on any of the plates. I never seen anybody eat so much food. Jessie had a cup of coffee.

"You feelin' better?" Jessie asked Rachel.

"Yes, thank you." Rachel patted her mouth with the napkin. Then she slid outta the booth and said she needed to go to the bathroom. Jessie hadda go to the bathroom, too, so they went together.

"Luke, you think we can get our money back from spy.com?"

"Uh-uh." Then he said, "Jessie went to the motor vehicle place, and Miss Sinclair gave her the address."

"How you know that, Luke?"

"She told me when we were waitin' in the car for you. I asked her how she got the address, and she told me."

"She say anything else?"

"Uh-huh." Luke took a sip of his chocolate malted. "She said she was proud of you."

"She said that?"

Jessie was walkin' toward the booth, and she looked at me and said, "Child, you musta eaten somethin' given you an allergic reaction. Your face is turnin' beet-red."

When we got back in the car, nobody said a word the whole trip to the hospital. When we got there, Jessie pulled into the parkin' lot. Rachel asked me if I would go in with her. I wasn't sure I should do that, but Jessie said I should, that she would wait in the car for me. I asked Luke if he wanted to go visit Charlie, and he said uh-uh, that he didn't wanna go in.

Just when me and Rachel started walkin', I turned to Rachel and asked her if she could wait a second, and I walked back to the car. Jessie rolled down the window. "What is it, sugar?" I leaned in and gave her the biggest kiss. "Thank you, Jessie. Thank you so much for doin' this."

Me and Rachel, we stopped in the ladies' room. She wanted to get herself lookin' nicer. She dumped everything that was in her purse into the sink and she found a rubber band to pull her hair back. Then she pinched her cheeks and made them all pink and healthy lookin'. She found some lipstick—a pretty pink color—puckered her lips, and put some on. She asked me if I wanted some. I said no thank you. Then she buttoned her sweater all the way up and turned to me.

"How do I look?" she asked.

"Pretty."

"Yeah?"

"Uh-huh. Real pretty."

When we got to the room, Charlie wasn't there. A sign over his bed said, IN THERAPY. I was awful glad he wasn't there. I don't know why, but I was. The curtain was all closed to Françoise's side of the room, and me and Rachel, we just stood there. It seemed like Rachel just froze stiff. Like one time, me and Luke, we were walkin' in the woods, and all of a sudden there was a bear. He was big and black, and I just froze. I felt like my legs were made of concrete. Then Luke, he was walkin' away real quiet, and he turned to me and he said, "Addie, don't just stand there lookin' at him. Come on." I never seen a bear that close before. That's what Rachel looked like, just standin' there frozen.

Then she turned and walked out of the room. She was leanin' up against the wall, right outside the door.

"I'm so scared, Addie, my hands are shakin'."

"I know. I'd be scared, too."

"You would?"

"Uh-huh."

I smiled at her, thinkin' that would make her feel better, which I guess it did, 'cause she started to walk back in. Then she gave me a look, the kinda look that says, *Please come with me.*

We were standin' right by Charlie's bed, and I said in a whisper that I'd be waitin' for her in the waitin' room and then she very quietly walked around the curtain. I stood for a few seconds, and I heard this voice, this woman's voice—it was so quiet, it was almost like a whisper—say, "I knew you'd come back."

When I was in the waitin' room, a coupla people came and went. They weren't there long enough for me to try and figure out why they were there. Mostly I was by myself. On top of the pile of magazines, there was a *Glamour* magazine, which I was glad about. I was lookin' at the pretty clothes and the pretty shoes when I felt someone enter the room. I looked up, and Sam was walkin' toward me. I closed the magazine and put it on the table and then I folded my hands on my lap. He didn't say anything. He sat down next to me on the couch. He looked at me. I looked at him. Then he took my hand and squeezed it. We sat for a few minutes sayin' nothin'. He just held my hand.

Then he turned to me and said, "Thank you, Addie."

And I said you're welcome, Sam.

chapter twenty-eight

Françoise died that night.

After me and Jessie got home, Jessie went right to the kitchen to make dinner, and I went up to my room. Durin' dinner, we didn't say a word to my dad about goin' to Marshalls Creek. Me, Jessie, and Luke, we sorta made a promise to each other that we would keep this our secret. We made that promise in the car, and we all crossed our hearts, even Jessie. My dad asked how my day was, and I said fine, just fine. Then he asked Jessie how her day was, and she said uneventful. She turned and winked at me, so I winked back. He told her he really liked the pork chops, and she said, "Thank you, Myles. It was my momma's recipe." Then Jessie and me we cleaned the kitchen. She washed and I dried. Then Jessie she went home.

I was up in my room, gettin' ready for bed, when the

doorbell rang. My dad said loud enough that I could hear him, "Wonder who that could be?" and when he opened the door, I heard him say, "Sam, what a surprise." I looked out my window, and I could see Sam Batalin standin' on our porch. My heart started poundin' real fast. My dad invited him in. I snuck out of my room and I sat down at the top of the stairs, so they couldn't see me, but I could hear everthing my dad and Sam were talkin' about.

Sam told my dad that Françoise had died and that she died in peace. My dad said a coupla times that he was sorry, real sorry, and that he always liked Françoise, and then he asked Sam if Sam wanted a drink, and Sam said no, thank you. Then my dad said, "I know how much you're gonna miss her." There was silence for a moment. Made me think about how one minute someone's alive and smilin' and talkin', and the next minute, they're silent and gone. Made me sad. Then Sam said he was grateful, very grateful. He asked where I was, and my dad said, "I think she's sleepin'," and Sam said "Well would you do me a favor, Myles, and thank Addie for me?" Then my dad asked how come you wanna thank Addie and then Sam told my dad all about Rachel, about me findin' her and everything, and that she was gonna stay with him for a while. He said how much he'd missed his little girl, and he was awfully glad to have her back.

"You have yourself a special little girl, Myles."

My dad didn't say anything, which made me think that he was noddin' his head.

It seemed like forever that Sam was in the house. Then I heard the door open and close. I tiptoed back to my room and closed the door real quiet. I looked out my window and I saw Sam leave. I could hear my dad walkin' up the stairs and then I heard him stop. I knew he was standin' right in front of my room. A few seconds later, I heard him walkin' down the hall to his room.

I opened my door and went down the hall. My dad was sittin' in his favorite chair. It's real big and old, and some of the stuffin' is comin' out of it. Jessie says it's not a chair, it's a chaise. She keeps sewin' it up, and it keeps rippin' open. He's had that chair for as long as I remember. He was readin' a book. When I said hi, he looked up, closed the book, and put it down on the night table.

"Can't sleep?" he asked.

"Uh-uh."

Then he scooted over and patted the chair. I climbed in and laid down right next to him. It's big enough for both of us. He put his arm around me. Last time my dad and me laid on the chair together, I was sick with a flu. I had chills and fever, and my throat was all sore and swollen. He told me a story till I fell asleep. I like him tellin' me stories better than him readin' me books. I like the way he tells 'em. And you know what else he did that time I was sick? He stayed with me all night, sleepin' right there next to me.

"Can you tell me a story, Dad?"

He looked at me and smiled. Then he rubbed his chin,

and I knew that meant he was thinkin' about what story he should tell.

"Okay, you ready?" I nodded. "His name was Fleming, and he was a poor Scottish farmer. One day, while tryin' to make a livin' for his family, he heard a cry for help comin' from a nearby bog. He dropped his tools and ran to the bog. There, mired to his waist in black muck, was a terrified boy, screamin' and cryin' and tryin' to free himself."

"What's a bog, dad?"

"A bog is like a swamp."

"Okay."

"Farmer Fleming saved that little boy from what could have been a slow and terrifyin' death. The next day, a fancy carriage pulled up to Fleming's farm. An elegantly dressed nobleman stepped out and introduced himself as the father of the boy Fleming had saved. 'I would like to repay you,' the nobleman said. 'You saved my son's life.'

"'I can't accept payment for what I did,' Fleming replied, waving off the offer.

"At that very moment, Fleming's son came to the door of the family cottage. 'Is that your son?' the nobleman asked.

"'Yes,' Fleming replied proudly.

"'I'll make you a deal. Let me take him and give him a good education. If that boy is anything like his father, he'll grow up to be a man you can be proud of.'"

"Like you're proud of me?" I asked.

"Yes, Addie, like I'm proud of you."

"Okay, go on."

"And he was so very proud of the man his son became. Fleming's son graduated from St. Mary's Hospital Medical School in London and went on to become known throughout the world as the noted Sir Alexander Fleming, the discoverer of penicillin. Years later, the nobleman's son was stricken with pneumonia. You know what saved him, Addie?"

"Penicillin?"

"That's right. And the name of the nobleman?"

I didn't know that. I just sorta shrugged.

"Lord Randolph Churchill. And you know who his son was?"

I didn't know that either.

"Sir Winston Churchill."

I knew who he was. I seen pictures of him in my history book. I felt good I knew that.

"You know what the motto of this story is, Addie?"

"Uh-uh."

"Sometimes a good is followed by a greater good."

epilogue

I'm tryin' to think of all the things that have happened since then.

Let's see, well, Rachel had a baby girl, just like Jessie said she would. She named her Françoise Addie Batalin. Rachel's been goin' to Stroudsburg Community College at night. She never went back to the creepy guy. Every coupla weeks, she sends me a letter with pictures of the baby. One time, right after New Year's, she and Sam and baby Françoise came by to visit. Rachel had cut her hair and lost a whole lot of weight, and she looked real pretty, and I told her so. Sam played on the floor with the baby and made all these funny noises, and the baby giggled and smiled, and I could tell that all of them were doin' fine, just fine.

Jessie bought me a training bra in bright pink. She gave it to me as a surprise one day. She handed me a small box that was wrapped real pretty, and she said, "Don't just stare at it, child. Open it. Come on, open it." It was all stretchy and the prettiest color pink I ever saw. I don't wear it every day, 'cause sometimes I forget to. But when I wear it, I feel all grown up.

Charlie and Joyce are livin' together again. They still fight like cats and dogs, but this time around, they make up real quick. Charlie's been doin' well. The doctor told him he hadda lose weight, and if I thought Joyce's food was awful before, it's even worse now. One night, I was over for dinner and she made this chicken thing. I asked her how come it didn't have no taste—it's like eatin' paper. She said it was 'cause she wasn't usin' salt anymore and then she said, "How do you know what paper tastes like, Addie?" And I said 'cause one time, I crumpled up a little piece of paper and chewed it and it had no taste.

"Yeah, baby, just like your chicken," Charlie said. Then he started laughin', but Joyce wasn't laughin', uh-uh. She got up from the table, opened the kitchen cabinet, took out one of those big cans of Diamond salt, and pounded it right down in the center of the table. Then she looked right at Charlie and said, "Don't you dare, Charlie. Don't you dare go near that. I want you stickin' around for a long time." Then she turned to me and Luke and said, "I don't wanna hear another word from you two 'bout my lousy cookin'."

Me and Grayce, well we sorta worked things out. Right after Françoise died, I went over to Grayce's house. I rode my bike there. I rang the bell, and she answered the door. She was surprised to see me. She asked me if I wanted to come in. I said I didn't need to come in. I just needed to ask her somethin'.

182

I said, "Grayce, would it be okay if me and you were friends? Would that be okay with you?"

Then she said she thought we were friends, and I said I didn't know that. How come I didn't know that? And she said 'cause I probably thought she was my dad's friend. That made sense, 'cause none of my dad's friends are my friends. I mean, I like 'em and everything, but I don't think of them as friends.

Then I walked over to my bike and started to get on it.

"I hope we can become good friends, Addie, real good friends," she called.

I got on my bike and started to ride away. Then I said real loud—real, real loud, "We could be good friends, but I already got a best one."

Then I rode to Luke's.